<u>Vengeance</u>

<u>By Jamie P Langridge</u>

For my Angela. Thank you for always believing in me.

Prologue

11th December 1980

It was cold and wet, as Barry made his long walk home. Barry looked like an ageing gangster despite being just 33. He had been down the pub with his friend Ray, his life was about to end, and Ray was the only person he could talk to. They had been mates for a few years now. Ray had gone to school with Barry's wife Tina. When they had met, they had resembled Frank Sinatra and Dean Martin. Whilst time had been kind to Ray who still had the same look of old blue eyes, Barry now wore the look of a football thug, but with the air of an old-fashioned gent. His hair was all but worn through, and his face was covered in scars from 3 years prior when he had managed to get himself on the wrong side of a knife, in a drunken brawl.

Barry considered himself a businessman, even if everyone else saw him as a brutal gentleman gangster. Everyone knew of the great Barry Denim, brought up by the head of an Italian mob, eventually recruited for his vicious mind as well as his intimidating muscular build, some respected him others feared him, the rest did both. Barry had never really understood the fear people felt for him, any violent crime he'd committed he'd done so to protect his family.

Tina sat at the table in her old-fashioned kitchen of her Chelsea home. It had been hard leaving South London, sure she and Barry had only moved a few miles but for Tina it was a huge move. She had left her father in the hands of her brother Santino. However here she was with Santino holding her twin boys. Santino wasn't a big man short with an average build. His thick black hair slicked back, the gel making his hair look even greasier than it already was. Tina shared the black hair although hers was soft and silky, rather than the greasy clump her brother now sported, as she did the nigh perfect olive-skinned complexion and finally the green eyes, which both her son's also shared with this Torellie gene.

"It'll be ok Tina. The boys are going to come live with me and Pops, I'm sorry but we've decided Barry can't be trusted to keep you all safe, trust me it's for the best." He'd informed her, the problem was Tina didn't trust her brother especially with the lives of her sons, but she was in no position to argue that with him now. Santino had arrived mob handed 3 bigger Italians waited in the hall, all dressed in fine expensive suits, and Tina knew they were waiting for her husband, and were all clearly armed. She knew Santino wouldn't hurt her, not while Barry still drew breathe, and the same went for her boys, but this meeting had a tense atmosphere. It was then Tina knew she and Barry had become dispensable for one reason or another, but Santino couldn't do any of this without her father's blessing, and deep down she knew he had it.

"Why Sonny?" she finally asked the words still quiet as if part of a secret conversation.   "It's strictly business Tina. It has to happen this way." He said it so coolly in a matter-of-fact way, and with a look at his watch, and a wave of his gold clad hand Santino left taking his hoods with him. Tina just sat there, fear rooting her to the seat she had occupied since Santino had first arrived.

It was 11:15pm by the time Barry climbed the three steps to his front door. The downstairs lights were on, he rested his shaven head on the oak door for a moment, before opening it. He knew deep down he'd fucked up. Barry had never worried who he crossed, had never backed down from anyone no matter how big, or important they thought they were. Now Barry had upset the wrong people. He'd found something on an organisation who were looking for a relationship with his father-in-law's company. Antonio had taken Barry in when he was just 14 years old, after the death of his mother. Barry had never known his father, Antonio had been the only man to resemble that position in his life, and now Barry knew he would be the one to give the go ahead for Barry to die. Barry walked into his home, the house was well kept, mainly by Tina. There was a small table by the front door overshadowed by a coat rack. Barry placed his keys and gun on top of it and walked through the hallway towards the kitchen where his wife Tina sat crying. Barry placed his large hand on her petit shoulder. "What's wrong baby?" the concern etched on his face. Tina told him about Santino, then came the words Barry hadn't wanted to hear.   "I thought they were going to kill us Barry, my father has given his blessing to have …..." Tina could see the fear wash over her husband's face, as her words drifted into nothing but tears and sobs, knowing he wasn't afraid for himself but for her.

"It's ok baby, you go upstairs bag up your things, I'll have Ray take you to my sister's place. Hopefully, I'll be enough."   "NO!" Tina tried to interrupt him, but Barry grabbed her other shoulder raising her up into his massive embrace.   "With me gone your dad can't sanction a hit on his own daughter, I have to do this we've no choice. Just look after our boys and know I love you all." He kissed her, placing his arms around her, enveloping her tiny frame in his massive build, both of them knowing it was likely to be their last embrace.

Whilst Tina packed Barry called Ray and set everything up, Ray wasn't happy he even spoke of getting some of the guys together, but Barry knew this was it, even if he survived the first attempt there'd be another and another, and no guarantee that he could keep Tina safe. This was the only way. As Tina rushed down the stairs two large holdalls in her hands, the doorbell rang. Barry looked at Tina as she dropped the bags, and they rolled down the remaining few steps. Barry nodded, surely it couldn't be Ray already, he picked up the gun he'd placed on the table earlier and opened the door. It wasn't Ray, it was a short man in a suit, holding a bible. "Hello sir, can I speak with you a moment about Christ our lord and savio......" the man didn't finish his sentence before his head vanished in a shower of blood, and slowly fell to the floor, it gave Barry the cover he needed to get the door closed, while he contemplated his next move. Then it was time to act. "Tina stays there! I mean it no matter what you wait for them to leave! I love you." Barry called to her before heading out the door. Tina stood on the stairs rooted to the spot. Fear coursed through them both, having opposite effects, as Tina's fear froze her in terror, Barry's fear just energized him. He felt the blood lust raise up in him, the adrenaline pumping and coursing through his veins. It pushed him, there was in that moment nothing else, but the feel of cold steel in hand.

The shooter sat across the road in his car. Aiming at the now closed door the target would show himself again, they couldn't leave the poor Christian he'd sent ahead as bait, to bring his quarry to him. Then it happened the man came out firing at the car, but he was shooting blind, giving his hunter the advantage of time to pick his shot.

Barry knew the shooter's rough position, but he also knew the shooter was already aware of his. He darted down the steps firing wildly hoping it was enough to put the shooter off. It wasn't. A shot rang out Barry saw the flash before he felt the impact. A searing pain ripped through his chest he knew it was bad as he hit the floor. He knew he was dead, his wound would prove fatal, but what now? If Tina did as she'd been told she could be ok but what if the shooter decided to check the house? Barry forced himself up into a sitting position leaning against a nearby car. It was then he saw the shooter still aiming at the door.

Tina heard the shots, each one sending a new wave of fear washing over her. She knew she couldn't stay paralyzed by this unsurmountable fear she felt, but what else could she do?

As Tina ran out into the cold night air. One shot rang out and Barry watched in horror as his wife's left eye disappeared into its socket, being replaced by a river of claret, before the back of her head exploded in similar fashion, and her slender legs gave way under the weight, which caused her to tumble to the floor, leaving her lifeless corpse in the street. It wasn't over Barry still had his gun, he'd failed Tina, he wouldn't fail James and Michael. His boys. His final thoughts.

The shooter dropped his head he hated to kill women, but it had to be done, but the man he wasn't dead yet. He would probably have his gun trained on his hunter by now, the shooter turned along with his gun towards the wounded man. He was raising his gun in the assassin's direction, but not quickly enough. The shooter fired this time aiming for the man's head.

The bullet struck Barry just above the cheek bone, killing him instantly. His body toppled over into the road and laid still. The job was done the shooter vanished into the night, with nothing left behind to incriminate him it would just be another long night for the metropolitan police. They'd never find a thing to link this back to him or his boss, and that was that. Just another shooting in fair old London town. Another dream washed away. Two more lives lost and wasted.

Chapter 1

27 years later

It was raining hard outside yet another great British summer evening. I lit another Benson as I awaited my next call of business.

His name was Reg Turnbull. Unfortunately, I knew this horrible junkie piece of shit. We went to school together; I'd always hated him. To be honest I hated all the fucking junkies. The only thing that made Reg any different to the rest of the junkie fucks, was Paulie Shawcross. My current side line employer.

Paulie was not the nicest fucker going, and Reg had upset Paulie somewhat. You see Reg was supposed to be knocking out a variety of drugs for Paulie. Thing was Paulie hadn't seen any return from Reg in 2 months. Now it came down to me to get £15,000 out of Reg, somehow.

Reg knew the score, I'd met him last week to inform him of his debt, and the possible reprisals for an inability to pay. I didn't care how he got the money. He could've robbed a fucking bank for all I cared, I just wanted that 15k.

As I stood there in the pissing rain, the black hoodie I was wearing soaked through, it felt like I was on sentry duty again. I'd been in the paras for 7 years. I left 2 years ago, but still should've been used to this. The thing is I'm not what you'd call a patient person. I hate waiting. Now Reg was taking his sweet, arsed time! Half an hour I'd been stood here soaking up the rain, like a fucking lemon. Reg was due 15 minutes ago. I knew then he wouldn't have the money. I decided to give him another 10 minutes, then I'd go to him.

Five minutes later I saw him walking up the road towards me. I knew I was going to give him a kick in now, money or not. He quickened his pace almost breaking into a run towards me. He was carrying a holdall; I could only assume this was the money.   "Jimmy sorry I'm late, I er got held up." Reg was a typical looking fucking junkie. Skinny Gaunt looking mother fucker. He was unshaven, but not to the point of having an actual beard. His brown hair was long, unkempt and greasy. "Never mind your shit time keepin' let's get in the dry!" I ordered him into the hotel I'd picked for the drop off. I was careful to keep my black baseball cap on, just in case things went south.

It was a plush setup. This was definitely not your average roadside b and b. There was a counter central to the foyer. Off to the left of which was a small coffee bar. I directed Reg into the café area.
"Two coffees Cheers guv." I called over to the guy serving, being sure not to get so close to give him a good look at my face. Then we sat in the corner as far out of sight and earshot of the hotel staff.
"So, the money then Reg." I asked, he simply lifted the holdall onto the table.

"It all in here Reg? No nasty surprises waiting for me?" I asked this time wanting an answer. "Yeah, it's all there. No surprises." He replied.

I watched Reg as the coffees arrived. Once our tender had left, I opened the holdall.   "Don't mind if I count it do ya Reggie?" I asked. "Not at all Mr Torellie. You do what you have to." He answered with a big smile on his face.

I peered into the holdall. As I did, I got that feeling in the pit of stomach. You know the one, the one that's telling you "This shit ain't right". Then screams at you "get the fuck out of it NOW!" But for some reason it's always too late.

The holdall had about 2 grand worth of twenties, only 13k short, the rest was shredded paper. What the fuck was Reg thinking? As I looked up at him, I realised. He had a gun pointed at my head. The junkie fucker actually thought he could shoot me and fuck off.   "Now Reggie mate, how are you thinking this plays out? I asked.
"I will shoot you Jimmy." He informed me. Well, that was me told, wasn't it?   "Will you?" I asked as he tried to direct me out from the table and into the foyer. I glanced over at the young guy at the counter. Fear was evident on his face, and he was definitely calling the police. I had to deal with this quickly.   "Just shut up and keep moving." Reg instructed, so I did raising my hands into a submissive posture, but there was nothing submissive about my intentions.
"You know, we might have a problem over there." I indicated towards the young lad at the counter. In that split second that Reg glanced over, I grabbed his gun hand with my left hand forcing it to arch to the right way from me. I only had one chance, so I had to get this right first time, otherwise I was dead. A shot rang out, he missed I raise my right hand to my left pressing his gun hand into a swan neck position, the gun now out of harm's way. I

launched a hard kick into Reg's groin, he doubled over, and I pulled down hard on his wrist. He staggered forward, completely off balance. He fell hard on his face. That was when he released the gun I grabbed it, pointing it straight at Reg.   "You stupid fuckin' junkie cunt!" Reg stared at the floor.

"Jimmy I'm sorry can't we talk …." He didn't finish as I unleashed to bullets into his skull. I dropped the gun grabbed the holdall, and left keeping my face down, and out of sight. It was a good thing I hadn't touched the coffee and hadn't yet removed the black leather gloves I wore on all of these sorts of jobs. It was always best to be careful.

I stepped out into the car park. Turning the corner, I'd parked my car a good ten-minute walk away from the hotel. As I turned the corner, I pulled my baseball cap off placing it in the holdall, then the same with the hoodie I had been wearing. The rain still pouring, I climbed into my Rover 75. It was a beautiful car top of the range. It was metallic blue, with a cream leather interior, and a wood grain dash. I whacked the heating on full, hoping maybe the white t-shirt I was wearing now would dry quickly. Then I sped away from the whole mess. Just another gangland shooting in London.

It took me 20 minutes to get to Paulie's gaff. I loved Paulie's house; it was a real gangster's paradise. It was one those stately homes, 8 bedrooms, and done in a Victorian style.

I'd always liked Paulie, he was an ageing gangster in his mid-fifties, yet still demanding a massive amount of respect. Paulie's face was a bit of a mess he had a couple of scars, and his nose had been broken more than a few times. All that said though he was never short of an attractive 20 something girl or two on his arm. In fact, they quite frankly adorned the walls of his house. I had no delusions they were foreign prostitutes, but that was Paulie's business and I stayed out of it.

I walked up to the door. The grounds really were something. A gravel driveway with small shrubs leading up to the house. Harry was stood minding the front door as usual.   "Alright Jimmy how was it?" Harry knew everything that went on in Paulie's empire.   "Not good Harry, the fucking junkie only had 2 g's! Then he only had the gall to pull a gun n try to top me!" I explained, still surprised at that turn of events myself.
"Fuck mine! Never thought he'd have the minerals to try something like that." Was all Harry offered in response?
"So, where's Paulie" I asked, I knew I was going to be in the shit but fuck it.   "He's in his office Jim, just go straight through mate." So, I did.

It was a fair walk to Paulie's office. I shit you not this place was an absolute fucking palace. It was like something out of the fucking Godfather films. I stopped in front of the door and regained my composure. I'd never fucked up like this before. I knocked on the old-style oak door. It opened immediately. Frank stood in front of me. Frank was a big lump, and Paulie's personal minder. He wasn't too handsome. To be fair that could've been because he was very good at his job. He'd taken at least 5 bullets and been stabbed about a dozen times, in the line of "duty". Frank like Paulie, and most of the lads, was old school in his fifties. "Jimmy how's things? You sorted that missus of yours out yet?" Frank asked with a chuckle. "I'm not too bad Frank, and that's ex-missus, and no not sorted her just yet." I informed him chuckling to myself. "For fuck sakes Frank! Let him in would ya? Oh, and do us a favour, wait outside for a bit." Paulie commanded from behind his massive desk. Frank as always did as he was told.

Paulie started to pour out two whiskeys.   "You stayin' for one Jim?" He asked knowing my answer.
"Yeah, why not." I sat opposite Paulie as he passed me a double measure.   "So, what happened son?" Paulie stared straight at me; I pulled the holdall up to the table emptying the contents over the table.
"He showed up with this holdall. That's what he gave me." I could see Paulie growing agitated. "What did you do Jim?" Make or break time. With my next few words, I'd be Paulie's golden boy, or pushing up daisies next to Reg.
"I shot him." Honesties the best policy and all that.
"You fuckin' did what? What are you FUCKIN' DIRTY FUCKIN' RAPE MY ARSEHOLE 'ARRY?!" Maybe not. So, I explained what had happened. "I did what I had to do Paulie. He didn't give me much choice. If it weren't for me, you wouldn't have got a penny." I reminded him.
"Alright Jimmy. Fair play. Your right I guess but do me a favour. Don't ever come in here trying to piss in my pocket and tell me it's raining again! That said you will get me the

rest of my money! I'm giving you a week! A man like you can locate £13,000 in a week, I know you fuckin' can. So do not fuck me again alright?" Fuck that went well.

I told him I'd sort it. I had to be honest, I could be a lot worse off, and God knows I'd got myself out of stickier spots. Fortunately, Paulie was right I'd have no problems finding the money. Whether or not I'd want to part with it, however, was another question entirely.

Chapter 2

"How did this happen?" Thought Stuart to himself, as he walked through Soho. Stuart was a bank manager for a major city bank. His son had been snatched a week ago but had been returned just three hours later with a note. It had read: -

Mr Greenslade

You will be aware by now, that your son Karl has spent 3 hours in our company. If you want this to be a one-off occurrence, we suggest you deliver us the sum of £250,000. If this amount is not paid, or you contact the authorities we will take your son again! And this time we won't be such tentative caring babysitters! We will call with location for payment.

He had been £50,000 short of the first drop and hoped this would be enough as he had followed all the other demands. It wasn't. As soon as Stuart had arrived home from the drop, He had found his wife bound and gagged on the sofa. Another note was resting on her chest.

Mr Greenslade

We tried being reasonable. Maybe we weren't clear enough. Be sure Karl is with us and will remain that way unless you pay us a further £300,000, that's the fifty you missed plus a further two fifty! Same drop point, AND NO POLICE! Please do not fuck us about again or Karl will be returned with a few scrapes and no pulse! You have 4 days till drop!

So here he was walking through Soho with a duffle bag filled with £300,000 in fifties. Again, he found himself asking. "How did this happen?" The girl at the front desk had given him a funny look when he asked, for the exact same ticket as four days previously. He thought of complaining to her manager, but he wouldn't be coming back regardless of the service. All that mattered was getting Karl back.

He walked down the theatre aisle and took his seat. There was a note on the back of the chair in front: -

Mr Greenslade

Please place the money behind your seat. Remain facing the screen if you move you and Karl are dead! Enjoy the film.

Stuart did as instructed. He waited for fifteen minutes. Then without warning a gloved hand covered his mouth, wrenching his head back muffling his terror filled scream. That was followed by the pain in his back. Something sharp had shot in and out of his back, then he saw what it was. A now blood-soaked hunting knife came down over his face, until it rested on his throat. Then with one swift movement, his attacker made the cut, and it was done. Stuart struggled for breath for a moment, but inevitably fell into deaths final embrace.

Chapter 3

I got back to my flat in Peckham around midnight. The garages had been full of the usual scumbags. Sometimes I wondered why I came back here. Don't get me wrong, even the worst shits round here don't give me too much hassle. You see they all knew Paulie. I suppose you could say he was a bit of a celebrity around the estate. Paulie grew up here, it was where he made his bones all those years ago. Back then times were different, you didn't meet many real gangsters. Now everyone wanted in on the action, everyone was on the take. More and more kids were trying to get into the gangster trade, but there were still the old guard in place, adapting with the times more than happy to take these kids under their wings. Training kids in the art of crime.

Me, I had different reasons for getting involved in this life. It wasn't really me. I'm not a Paulie Shawcross. Alright I'm not averse to ending someone's life, if it's needed, I was in the army for Christ's sake, and I was just hired muscle, nothing more. It really was just a release for me, I took the job with Paulie when my then wife left me and took our daughter.

So, I traversed the stairs of my tower block, to my second story two bed flat. I always took the stairs, I don't trust lifts, especially the ones on this estate. As I opened the door, I pulled off my t-shirt tiredly. The smell of stale smoke hung in the air. I walked into the kitchen and opened the fridge. It was empty except for the two cans of Stella and a half-eaten pizza from the night before. The kitchen was immaculate. Something I contributed to me not using it very often. The past year I had survived on takeout and alcohol. Tonight, would be no different.

I had two messages on my answerphone. I hit play. "Hi this is Jimmy's phone, I'm not in. Probably on the piss. Leave a message after the tone, or hang-up and stop wasting my time." I should really change that message. "First message" The machine informed me. "Hi bro it's Michael. Just checking in to see how you're doing today. Give me a call and we'll meet up. Speak to ya later." My brother Michael the only person who didn't know about my employment with Paulie. Good thing to, as Michael was a detective sergeant in the met, CID. He was also my twin brother and one of my only surviving family members, our parents were killed when we were just 6 months old, we'd lived with our grandfather until he passed 15 years ago. The only other family we had left was our Uncle Santino.

"Second message" God these machines were on the ball. "Jimmy its Liz. I need to know what time to drop Lacey off on Saturday. Call me and let me know. Thanks." Ah the estranged wife. I'd call them tomorrow.

As I walked into the living room, I flicked on the light, I saw a half empty bottle of Jack Daniel's, sitting centre stage on the coffee table. As I picked it up, I realised it was guarding two framed photos of my two absent families. One was taken just two years ago, it was the day I'd got back, after leaving the Army. We were all so happy that day I can't remember who took that photo, but it had been one of my favourites. I looked a hell of a lot better back then. Short cropped brown hair, military issue. I was clean shaven and looked a lot younger than I did now. Now I looked every bit the 28-year-old ex-squaddie that I was. My green eyes framed by a pair of heavy bags, my hair long swept back, and the long goatee beard that I wore more as a way to hide my face. Liz had looked stunning as she always had, she was fairly tall, largely down to her devilishly long legs. With her long brown hair and slim figure, she could've had any man she wanted. I was amazed that for 3 years at least, I had been that man. Her best feature as far as I was concerned though, were her luscious blue eyes. The beautiful blue eyes that seemed to dance with happiness or light up the darkest room.

On her lap was my daughter Lacey she was only a 2 at the time, her hair was blonde her green eye's a family trait from my side of the family. I knew as much as I hated to admit it, like her mother in years to come Lacey would become something of a heartbreaker. It wasn't long after that Liz had cheated on me with some no mark P.E teacher from a local school.

In the other photo was my other family, a more tragic story, it was a picture of my first wife Angela and my son Bexley. The picture was about 8 years old, taken a year before they had both been killed in an RTC. Angela was beautiful, I had to admit I'd been relatively lucky with women, even then I hadn't really thought I was that good looking, but the women I had been with had been stunning. Angela was shorter than me, short brown hair and brown eyes you could drown in. Bexley was only 3 at the time but looked just like me. In this picture I was still in my uniform, it had been taken just after my passing out parade, I'd just received my red beret.

I was also a bit of an arsehole back then. I loved Angela I really did, but I was a cheating bastard. It was a lesson I learnt, but back then I just couldn't help myself. It sounds stupid I know, here I was with a beautiful woman, despite not being the best-looking bloke myself, but Angela had been my first and only girlfriend. We'd been together since school, we were only 17 when she'd fallen pregnant with Bexley, and so I had felt I'd missed out on my days of playing the field, even more so when I joined the army.

So maybe deep down I could accept I had deserved what Liz had done to me. After all I had cheated on Angela several times, in our 6 years together. Now Liz lived in my house in Downham, with Warren the no mark P.E teacher. A now balding 35-year-old. Whilst I sat alone, most nights, in my two-bed flat in Peckham getting drunk.

After I left the army, I had set up my business. The work I did for Paulie had been one of the side effects from that. The business was a private security agency. I'd gone into partnership with one of my mates from the para's. Ali Smith, or Smithy as we'd called him, was a top bloke, and one hell of a soldier. He had to be medically discharged after being injured in Armagh Northern Ireland.

Ali was a big guy too. I mean I'm of average height at 6"1 but Ali dwarfed me, by an easy foot. He was also built like a brick shithouse. I've never been in any doubt if I was going into a situation where I'd need backup, Smithy was who I wanted to have my back. Even now 3 years on from his M.D Smithy looked every bit the soldier he had been. He was always clean shaven with his blonde hair neatly cropped. Ali wasn't just my business partner he was my best mate.

Smithy however wasn't my only business partner though. We had struggled in the first year, and Paulie had bailed us out. Now me and Ali owed him and until we'd paid him with interest, I worked off the debt. Which had just increased by £13,000.

So that was my life it wasn't great, but it wasn't as bad as it could be. Me and Michael had never known our parents, we didn't even know they're first names. Come to think of it we didn't know for definite, that they had chosen to name us Jimmy and Michael. We had flitted between care homes from the age of 13. Safe to say no one really wanted us around back then.

I swigged at the Jack and lit a smoke. As I did, I made a decision. No more self-pity. Life could have been a lot worse. I needed to get back in shape. I'd let myself go a bit over the last year. Another 2 hours and I'd black out.

The sun light crept through the curtains. The beam of light ran across my face. I opened my eyes and allowed the world to slowly come into focus. I looked at the clock on my phone, it was 6:30. Great I had two and a half hours to kill before meeting Ali down the café. An opportunity to put my late-night resolve into action I thought. So, I neatened up my goatee, I'd become quite fond of it so didn't want to shave it off completely, I Hit the weights, dropped down for 20 press-ups, then left the flat for a twenty-minute run round the block. The run turned into a ten-minute run and a twenty-minute walk back, I really was out of shape.

I got to the café bang on 9:00, as usual Ali was there waiting. I took the seat opposite him. I saw the shock on his face. "Fuck me, you look almost respectable this mornin'! What happened you shit the bed?" He said chuckling to himself.   "No, I just decided it was time I sorted myself out." I felt a sense of pride at picking up the pieces of my shattered life. "Seriously? Who are you and what have you done with the real Jimmy?" He asked sarcastically. Before I had a chance to respond, one of the café's young waitresses came over to our table. I let my stare linger to long, Ali being one of those blokes that always loved a wind up noticed instantly. "Ah so sorting yourself out means getting laid as well!" He laughed hysterically. Some of the builders looked over with accusatory stares.

The waitress wasn't a bad looking girl, but the manner in which she carried herself wasn't flattering her at all. I myself would've put her at about 18 maybe 19, that being said, working here she was probably younger. She had long brown hair, which looked greasy but working in a greasy spoon, what did you expect. She had a great figure. Yet her eyes were dull and uninterested.

The worst thing about this bored beauty, whom was obviously trying to be unattractive, was the gum. She sounded like a cow chewing a cud. As I said you could trust Ali to spot a wind up a mile away. As she leant on to our table Ali's eyes lit up. "'Ello treacle. We'll have two big breakfasts, two coffees and my buddy 'ere would love your digits!" My jaw dropped. The fucker was trying to set me up with a fucking schoolgirl! She gave it me as well as if I was actually going to call her.

It was then I noticed four lads on a table by the counter, all about the same age as the waitress. All four were glaring at me and Ali. This would end badly! They all stood up and marched over to us. I knew where this was going. The little boys would give it some mouth show how big they were, and the sensible adults, who knew better and were outnumbered, apologised and allowed the kids their little victory. One small problem with that scenario. Ali and I, we're not sensible adults, we're ex-squaddies.

The bravest lad knelt beside Ali; the kid looked like bloody Micky Pierce off only fools. Ali simply looked at me. I nodded then turned to the lads. "Is there a problem boys?" I questioned emphasizing the word "boys". I watched as the toe rags eyed Ali, as if sizing him up. "Yeah, I want to know, what this tubby fuck, said to my girl!" Micky stated. That was it Ali's fuse was lit. He glared at the brazen little bastard. "I asked her for her number. Oh, and I ain't tubby half pint!" Ali informed the little up start. Then as if to prove his size had nothing to do with pies and burgers, he tensed his arm. "Is that supposed to scare us old man?" Another lad said as he stepped up. I could see Ali getting agitated. These little cunts were searching for their little victory. Well, I had news for them. They weren't going to get it!

I stood up and stepped towards Micky Pierce. I kicked his leg, he looked up at me in confusion. "Hi mush, just so you know your little girlfriend gave me her number! If you've still got a problem, I suggest you and your mates meet me outside, and I'll smear you all over the pavement!" I watched as the little twats walked out. They stopped at the doorway. I felt the smile spread across my face. I looked at Ali. "I've got this one mate." I told him as I headed for the door.

As I stepped through the door Pierce was waiting. He launched a punch, I caught it in the jaw. I licked the blood from my lip, I didn't mind admitting it was a good hit, even if it was incredibly cheap. I stepped back smiling at the lad opposite Micky. He was an ugly fucker. He had ginger hair and freckles, he was short and stocky. His eyes were squinty, and he was covered in acne. Ginge looked at me in confusion, I spun and head-butted Micky. He dropped like a sack of spuds. The other three watching. I saw the fear creeping into their expressions. "Anymore for anymore?" I asked I didn't get an answer, they picked up Micky and left.

I turned to re-enter the café, when I was punched again. This time the punch was harder, and I could feel the experience and strength behind it. I think I actually felt my brain rattle around my skull. I dropped to my knees. I had to regain my bearings. Then I heard a voice shouting at me, it was a Manchurian accent. "GET UP NOW YA FUCKER! I'LL NOT HITCHA DOWN THERE YA FUCKIN' SOUTHERN FAIRY!" I looked up the voice belonged to a fella Ali had been investigating. He was a big lump to, skinhead type. He was definitely a bloke used to the odd fist fight.

His name was Graham Dixon. I tried to stand up, but my legs felt like jelly. Seeing me struggle, Graham decided to help me up. That's when I saw his right-hand hurtling towards me. I raised both arms up to block the punch, but I wasn't quite fast enough, and the punch rocked me again. Once I'd realised who he was, I wasn't at all surprised I was wavering the way I was. Graham Dixon was a retired, heavy hitting, heavyweight boxer. I allowed my eyes to focus and readied my counterattack.

I was too late; I heard a massive crash. Immediately I knew what it was. I used the wall of the café to help myself up. I looked round and saw Ali had successfully wrestled Mr. Dixon to the ground, and into submission. My head was spinning and was struggling to concentrate, as I tried to figure out why I'd just taken a two-punch pounding. I felt the blood filling my mouth, I spat it out onto the pavement. The only thing going through my head, "what the fuck did I do this time?" Eventually Ali defused the situation. Then he led me, and Mr. Dixon across the street to the office.

It turned out Mr. Dixon's wife had hired Ali to find out if Mr. Dixon had been cheating on her. Simple answer he wasn't. What he was doing was the same as his wife, except the P.I he was using wasn't very good. He'd seen me giving Ann Dixon the news that her husband was faithful. Mrs Dixon was 24 and it had to be said quite a tasty sort. She'd been so pleased her marriage was safe she had kissed me, on the cheek, needless to say at the wrong angle that would look a lot different. Mr. Dixon had been shown a picture of said wrong angle, which I guessed could sort have explain my recent pasting.

It was Mr. Dixon that started the discussion. "I'm sorry about that pal!" "Hindsight's a wonderful thing." I answered steadily, hiding the pain he'd caused to my face, and pride. So much for the new image I thought, as I felt the tell-tale throbbing, of my face blowing up like a balloon. "Jesus that looks fucking painful, I am so sorry." Dixon started again. "It's fine. So how much did our competitor charge you?" I had to ask I'd taken two professional punches for it. He took some time to think then he told me. "Fuckin' hell! We would have done a better job for half that!" was all I could say, Dixon just looked at me. "Hindsight's a wonderful thing." He informed me.

We chatted for a bit and Mr. Dixon paid us what we had originally charged his wife. "For damages caused." He'd said as he signed the cheque.

As Dixon left, I heard the office phone ring. Ali reached it first. "Hello Torellie and Smithy security and investigations limited, how can I help you?" Ali loved all that professional stuff. He paused a while allowing the potential customer time to speak. "Yes of course sir." Ali looked up pointing the phone in my direction. "Said he wants you." I heard the pang of disappointment in his voice.

I took the phone from Ali and gave him a reassuring nod. "Hello, Jimmy Torellie here. How can I Help today?" I asked. "Er yes Mr. Torellie My names Greg Wyman. I need your help to find my daughter, she's been kidnapped. I will pay you £50,000 to find her." Wyman informed me. "Okay. Mr Wyman I must ask you, have you contacted the Police?" Well, I didn't want to step on any toes. "Yes, fat load of good they've been. Lazy bastards!" He told me. "Okay Mr Wyman. I'll come round to your house tomorrow morning, then ask you some preliminary questions, and we'll go from there." I told him my head was still pounding, I needed to get off home. "Fine." Wyman snapped. "Just one thing Mr Wyman. Why did you want me to do this? I mean why me specifically?" I asked, I was intrigued to know why Ali wasn't good enough. "Because I knew your parents and I thought I could help you, if you helped me." Stated Wyman. Shit. He knew my parents' maybe he knew what happened. I made the arrangements for the morning, and took his address, said goodbye and hung-up.

Ali looked at me. "So, what was all that about mate?" "He knew my parents. May know what happened to them." Ali looked on in shock at my last statement. Ali told me, he thought it would be best if I went home. "Go on mate just take the rest of the day off get some rest. You took some nasty blows to the head out there." He told me. I had to agree so I left the office and headed home.

Chapter 4

I contemplated going to see Lacey on my way home. I eventually decided that was a bad idea. I didn't much fancy spending a few hours with Liz and fucking Warren, watching over me waiting for me to snap. That being said as it turned out I would be spending time with all three.

I walked through the garages and saw her in the doorway of my tower block. I didn't look at her as I unlocked the door. "And to what do I owe this pleasure?" I asked sarcastically. I didn't mean to be hateful, I really didn't, I just didn't know how else to be. "Does it have to be like this all the time?" Liz asked I could hear the sadness in her voice. I felt a pang of guilt, but then I thought fuck it she cheated on me and took my daughter from me! What did she expect me to be like? "I don't know, maybe. I guess you'd better come up though." I let her through first. I still refused to allow myself to look at her face. So, she led the way up the dank staircase in her leggings and cashmere sweater.

It wasn't until I let her into the flat that I saw her face. For the first time since we'd met, she looked a state. She wasn't wearing any makeup. Her hair was dry and unkempt, with no effort made. Her left cheek was swollen along with her eyes. There was a cut on the bridge of her nose. To top it all off her lip was busted. "What the fuck happened to you?" I couldn't think, I'd never seen her like this. "I could ask you the same thing." Was all she said. I was getting frustrated. She'd obviously came to me to sort whoever had done this to her, but now she was here, she didn't want to talk about it. "Look I can't sort this, if I don't know who it was that hit you!" Then came the brick wall. "It was Warren." She stated as the tears started to well up in her swollen eyes. In shock at this revelation, I put my arm around her. "Was Lacey there?" I asked knowing the answer. "Yes" "And you've left her there?" My anger was building, I felt my arm tensing, "No, she's at the nursery." Thank Christ. "And she's still there?" I had to be sure, especially with what I had in mind for the no mark P.E teacher. That's when she kissed me.

I pulled my head away and shock my head. "No, that ain't happening!" I snapped. "I don't want you back Liz, you and me that's done, I got absolutely no intention of going there again!" Her eyes fell to the floor, I think this could've been the first time she'd ever been alone. "I'll look after you, for Lacey's sake but you and me won't work. Give me an hour I'll have this all sorted." I informed her as I left the room, I walked through to the kitchen, opening the top drawer on the chest by the oven, I lifted the cutlery tray, there laid my Gloch, with two mags full of ammo. I could feel Liz behind me before she managed to speak. "No Jim, you can't kill him!" I stopped myself from questioning her latest statement, but instead decided to reassure her. "It's not for that, it's just in case. I'm going in alone it's just to keep him on the level." With that I placed the Gloch in the back of my waistband and walked out the front door.

Chapter 5

Markus was escorted into the Klichkov Art Gallery. As always, he was directed around the metal detectors. Markus had just turned 60 although he could have passed for 40. His eyes were a piercing blue and his hair a fading blonde, cut short. He stood 6"6 with a strong build.

"Mr Krueger, how's business?" It was Klichkov himself. He always made the effort to greet Markus personally. "Very good, Gregor. Do you have anything for me?" He knew

Klichkov would, and no doubt it would cost him. "The Seventh Day, New this week there is much interest in this piece." It was quite magnificent thought Markus. "Very nice Gregor, I will pay, £70,000,000 now." Klichkov whistled through his teeth. "Done." This was always the way it worked, the German would make an offer and the Russian would up it by £10,000,000, and Krueger would always pay it.

Gregor was also close to 60 but wasn't ageing quiet as gracefully as Krueger. Klichkov was a portly fat cat. His hair obviously dyed black, along with his thick moustache. Both men wore expensive designer suits. Krueger's muscular frame giving him the better look.

Markus placed his Armani sunglasses on and turned to leave. "Ve has Lunch tomorrow discuss delivery." Markus was heading for the exit. "Of course, Mr. Krueger, I look forward to it."

Chapter 6

D.S Michael Torellie looked across at his partner, DC Kate Marshall. Kate was a very attractive woman. Her short hair pulled back tight in a ponytail, helped accentuate her face, along with her pale skin, and her eyes a deep blue. She was short but had a staggering figure. Michael looked just like Jimmy except his hair was cut shorter, and he was clean shaven.

"So how long did forensics estimate he's been dead?" Michael asked. "About three hours. Looks like it was a hunting knife, its gone straight through the seat." Kate responded "Well they either killed him before the movie started, or he wasn't here for pleasure. We got any I.D for him?" Michael didn't hold out much hope. "Mr. Stuart Greenslade, and the note uniform found on the chair in front indicates he wasn't here for the film." Michael knew there would be uniform at the house already, so next question. "Any prints?" "No, no prints, no witness', no DNA and no actual murder weapon." Kate stated. "Oh, a fun one!" Michael said already feeling exasperated by the lack of evidence in this case. It was one of those investigations. "Like trying to do a picture less jigsaw!"

A uniformed officer ran in. "DS Torellie, news from the victim's house!" "What is it then lad?" Michael was getting impatient. "His wife sir. She's been shot dead sir." "Let me guess, no evidence?!" Kate let it hang there more like a statement then a question, which both her and Michael would know the answer to. "No, not even ballistics." The young officer finally stated. "Fuck it! I'm going for a walk!" Michael headed down the stair aisle. "He does that, needs to clear his head." Kate informed the young P.C. They watched as Michael disappeared behind the screen. Seconds later they heard him scream.

"KATE, KATE! GET YOUR ARSE BACK HERE NOW!" Michael screamed, then he threw up. In all his years in the police he'd never seen anything as horrific as the scene that lay in front of him now! Kate ran in, "Oh my god," she staggered back. "God had fuck all to do with that!" Michael said dryly as he stared at the blank eyes of the young boy in front of him. The child could only have been 6 years of age. He'd been stripped and had thousands of cuts over his body. Then a crucifix had been carved out of his throat.

"I'm gonna get these fuckers Kate." "No Mike, we're going to get these bastards!" Kate told him, as he radioed for forensics.

Chapter 7

As I drove towards my old home, I felt the anger bubbling up inside me. How dare that cunt hit my wife? Okay we were separated, and neither of us wore our wedding rings, but I hadn't signed the divorce papers, so she was still my wife!

I pulled up opposite the house. As I stepped out of the car I looked over at my average sized terraced house. It had a typical look about it, with just the one window overlooking the London side road, from the ground floor. I'd painted the door blue before I'd moved out. Now it looked tatty as the weather beaten paint was peeling revealing brown flashes of oak.

I opened the gate and marched into the overgrown front garden. What the fuck did that prick think he was doing, no wonder Liz had always insisted on bringing Lacey to me. As Warren opened the door I was only halfway down the path, about 3ft from the door. "What's up Warren?" I asked my anger seeping through my voice.

Warren slammed the door, so I backed up to the gate, to give myself a run up. Using the momentum from my run up I kicked the door inwards. Warren was still in the hallway, his face a mix of shock and fear. "Why you scared Warren? You weren't scared of my wife, were you? No, you were the big man when you were knocking her about!" My voice resonated with malice, as I glared at him.

Warren raised his hands level with his chest and started walking backwards toward the living room. "It wasn't like that Jimmy, I swear if you let me explain..." I didn't let him finish, I surged forward. I was enraged that he felt he could justify what he'd done. "EXPLAIN WHAT YOU MUG? EXPLAIN YOU'RE A FUCKING COWARD!" I screamed as I slammed into him. The force carrying us both crashing to the floor, I allowed gravity to throw my head into his nose, which exploded on impact.

I jumped up and lifted him to his feet. I slammed him into the wall. "Once we're finished here, you're going to get your stuff and fuck off out of my house, and you're not going to come back! Under fucking stood!?!" I told him, he nodded furiously. "Good! Now how many times did you hit my wife?" I asked the fear spread across his face. "F-f-f-five." He sputtered the claret flowing from his nose. I let him go he started slipping to the floor, so I gave him a backhanded slap across his face. He staggered sideways, I grabbed him and slammed my fist into his gut.

As Warren doubled over, I smashed my knee into his ribs. He was shaking and crying, from fear and pain. I punched him hard in the jaw. He dropped to the floor in a semi-conscious heap.

"Now get up, get your stuff and fuckoff out of it!" I told him. He lifted himself up and staggered out into the hallway. I let him get on with it whilst I called Liz back at the flat. I told her I was going to pick Lacey up from the nursery, and I'd go over and pick her up once I'd fixed the door.

As I turned around Warren was stood in the doorway. He was holding a large kitchen knife. "YOU'RE NOT GOING ANYWHERE, AND YOU'RE NOT TAKING MY FAMILY FROM ME EITHER!" Warren screamed at me, his hand tightening around the knives' handle. I just looked at him and laughed. I had no doubt he was about to attempt to use the knife, but I couldn't help but laugh.

"WHAT'S SO FUCKING FUNNY?" He screamed at me. I pulled out the Gloch. "Well first off, they're not you're family, they're mine. Second, you've brought a knife to a gun fight, and thirdly, is the fact due to my time in the para's, I don't need the gun." I said calmly placing the Gloch on the TV unit. "I could disarm you of your knife and snap you're arm, without a moment's hesitation. Now I'm going to collect my daughter. You had better be packed and gone when I get back or fuck the unarmed combat training, I'll fucking shoot you. Now drop the knife and go get started!" I picked up the gun and pointed it at him, to show I wasn't fucking about.

Needless to say, Warren headed upstairs. I left to pick up Lacey, after I'd apologised to the neighbours for the noise, and asked them to watch the house for me whilst I was gone.

I only just reached the nursery on time. Largely due to the fucking London school run traffic. I'd forgotten how bad it was. I walked through to the main entrance, my eyes searching for Lacey, it was a small hall with a double door entrance. Lacey was in the foyer, I felt the smile spreading across my face, as my daughter spotted me and called out, as she ran across the hall towards me. I dropped to my knees as she ran into my arms, giving her old man a big hug.

Chapter 8

It took forensics just over an hour to reach the murder scene. It took half an hour for two special investigations officers to arrive on scene, a male and a female Michael didn't like her. She claimed to be with MI5 and knew the killer's M.O, although she was concerned the child was held for ransom. "He's called the Priest." Said "Agent" Daniels, "He normally targets Paedophiles and their victims, he snatches the child and kills them first then comes back for the Paedophile. He knows no-one will go to the police makes covering his tracks a lot easier." Her partner "Agent" Fuller informed Michael and Kate. They both spoke with calm tones normally used by top brass, but they we're both far too young to be that high up. "You've stumbled onto something quite interesting here DCI." Daniels finished. "I considered it sick myself Agent Daniels!" Michael almost spats the words. "Quiet, well you won't have to worry now as B.O.S 90 will be heading the investigation now. We've been looking for this guy for 3 years now and believe me he's slightly above your pay grade!" She stated with an air of grace that didn't sit with Michael, he recognised her but couldn't place her.

Agent Daniels was an attractive woman around the age of 26, she wore a tight fitting business suit, and how she could "fight crime" in that Michael was clearly unsure. Her long blonde hair has tied back in a bun, she looked like a secretary not a copper he thought to himself. Agent Fuller on the other hand had the poise of a military man, and a Rupert at that. He also wore a business suit, but Michael could see he could most definitely handle himself. He bore scars that could have been in the line of police duty or more likely a warzone. However, Michael didn't like being told he was off a case by a branch of MI5 he'd never heard of.

By the time forensics were finished they had a good idea what had happened chronologically, the child had been dead for some 12 hours, his father just a few hours. It certainly fitted the Priest's M.O, but what that meant for Michael and Kate was anyone's guess. This B.O.S 90 were now in full flow bagging and tagging the bodies, not taking much in way of evidence, which pissed Michael off even more than they're original intrusion. However, he would have to wait for answers, as him and Kate's superiors' were on the radio now instructing them to head back to the station and finish up for the day.

Chapter 9

I dropped Lacey off at my flat, where her Mum was waiting. I still had a lot to do, and not a lot of time to do it. I called Ali at the office and explained what had happened over the last few hours. "So, you have all the fun again." He told me laughing. We agreed to meet at the house to fit a new door, and make sure Warren had in fact fucked off. Then I called Mike, he was busy with a case, but agreed to come over once his shift was done.

Once Ali and I had fitted the door, I left him fitting some CCTV cameras he'd brought over from work, whilst I collected Lacey and Liz. By the time we got back Ali had already helped himself to a beer. I decided to join him. I put a film on for Lacey whilst myself, Ali and Liz chatted.

Michael arrived at 20:00. It had been difficult for me to talk to Michael since I'd started my part time job, but the time was coming when I thought I'd have to come clean, and deal with the consequences. Michael made a big fuss of

Lacey as he always had, she was our little princess, and we both made a point of making sure she knew it.

I put Lacey to bed about 20:30, she was still a bit excited at having both her Dad and Uncle around, but eventually she had gone off to sleep. When I got downstairs, they were all sat in the living room. Michael and Ali were drinking Lager, with Liz sat opposite them both holding a large glass of red wine. The stereo, sat between the sofas at the end of the room, was playing "Lionel Ritchie" at a soothingly low volume. I cracked open a can and sat on the arm chair in the corner of the room. As I took my sip of the fresh Lager, there was a loud bang on my new front door.

The noise had obviously woken Lacey as she called down the stairs. "Liz goes see to Lacey. Jim, Ali with me!" Instructed Mike, I was already racing through the hallway. Liz ran upstairs, ushering our Daughter back to her room. I was already outside followed closely by Michael and Ali. I couldn't fucking believe it, it was Warren and four other blokes. "Warren what the fuck is your damage?! I told you to fuck off and leave my family alone!" I glared at him. I heard Ali behind me. "Finally, I get some fun, about fucking time!" he smiled. Then just as the five trespassers were about to kick off, a big white van pulled up. It took me a few seconds to realise, it was the Police.

In a moment they were out of the van and rounding everyone up. A few officers even came over to arrest the three of us, until Michael flashed his warrant card. "Oh, fuck sorry about that sir." Said one of the younger coppers. Once it was all over, we all headed back to the living room, where Lionel had been softly warbling to himself, and tried to enjoy the rest of our evening.

Michael eventually admitted he had, had a car following Warren since my earlier call. I sat silent for a moment, the thought of work got me thinking. "Mike, I've got a case I think you should know about." I finally stated. I then proceeded to explain the Wyman case and its possible interest.

"Mum and Dad knew this Greg Wyman then?" Michael asked. "Yeah, and now his Daughters gone missing." I thought for a second and then it hit me. "So, you've not heard about this case?" I asked Mike. "Never heard of anyone called Wyman." He stated. Ali jumped in. "So, he must be lying about your lots of involvement then?" Liz looked at the three of us individually. "What makes you think that?" She questioned. "Well." I spoke. "He asked for me by name, if as he says he'd gone to the Police, knowing Mike was there, surely, he'd of asked for him. Do us a favour Mike." I continued. "Get me a background check on this Wyman. Cause I'm hearing some, loud fucking alarm bells ringing now." I wasn't sure, but there was most definitely something fucking wrong with this picture! Michael protested, he could get into some serious shit with his top brass, for passing information on a member of the public, but I assured him. "I just want to know what I'm getting myself into." Michael seemed to accept this as his brotherly duties. "Alright I'll see what I can pull up."

With that Michael left after telling me, not to go to Wyman's until he called tomorrow. I told him I wouldn't, and he went home. Ali left himself, shortly after, then Liz and I finished our drinks, and set up a bed on the sofa. "You don't have to sleep there. It's okay you can stay upstairs I won't try anything." Liz told me. "It's okay I'm used to sleeping on sofas, I don't think I could sleep in a bed anymore." I added. We shared a smile, said goodnight, and Liz headed up to bed.

Chapter 10

In the morning I left the house, safe in the knowledge Warren would still be in the cells. I said goodbye to Lacey, telling her I'd be back later, and headed for the café to meet Ali as usual. The whole time thinking about the Wyman case. I don't know why, but I couldn't allow myself to wait for Michael to get back to me, maybe it was the idea of a young girl being missing, maybe I was just getting punchy. I gave Ali Wyman's address and told him to find me if Mike called with information suggesting Wyman being less than harmless.

On the drive to Wyman's place, I kept wondering how he had known my parents. Did he know who killed them? Did he know what happened to Michael and my inheritance? Had our Uncle really absconded with it? If he, hadn't it would suggest our parents had spent their nights in a cardboard box outside Kings Cross.

I quickly found Wyman's house on Anerley Road. The place was a shithole. I parked up across the road, to check my gun.

From the moment Wyman opened the door I took an instant dislike to him! Greg Wyman was a fat, smelly old man. He looked to be in his 70's yet it became clear it wasn't his age, nor the ravages of time that was causing his appearance. It was in fact the same things that were slowly destroying my body from the inside out, that said I was fairly sure I smoked and drank a tad more moderately than this degenerate. As I begrudgingly shook his hand, I could smell the vodka on his breath. Christ it wasn't even 9am!

I decided to make this quick and contact social services. There was no way I was bringing a 12 year old girl back to this hovel. I asked the more obvious questions first. It didn't help my first impressions. It took twenty minutes for Wyman to tell me, Christine Wyman was a 12 year old girl, who had lost her Mother ten years ago. She also never had any friends back after school, I couldn't fucking blame her! Finally, I asked for a recent picture of Christine, it would ultimately be more helpful if I knew what she looked like. As soon as Wyman had retrieved the picture, that feeling this case was going to get very fucked up very fucking quickly returned.

Greg as I said looked older than he probably was. This was because he was bald, fat and dressed like he belonged in the fifties. His nose and cheeks were a rosy red, and he had grey stubble around his mouth. All in all, he looked like Santa from a council estate, but without most of the beard. However, I took issue with Christine's photo. Christine was a typical looking 12 year old girl, with her black curly hair in braids. She was slim with petit delicate features. The problem I had was, unlike her father, Christine was black!

Chapter 11

"Ali, its D.S. Denim." Michael announced.

"Alright Mike mate. What's up?" Ali responded in his usual cheery manner.

"I've done that check for Jimmy. Is he there at all?" Mike asked.

"No, he's down at Wyman's place, why?" Ali replied to confusion clear on his voice. Mike answered angrily.

"He's what? For fuck sakes! He said he wanted a check done before getting into this case. Jesus! Right, Ali can you get over there?" Mike sounded nervous, this put Ali in a state of unease.

"What is it mate? What did you find?"

"I'm not sure but Wyman's not telling the truth. He doesn't have any children." Michael informed him.

"What's all this about then? Why'd he wants Jimmy to investigate his Daughter's kidnapping if she doesn't exist?" Ali was well and truly confused, none of this made any sense.

"I've got no idea, It does explain why he didn't come to the police, but I think it's best you get Jimmy out of it now." Ali suddenly realised he'd forgotten being given this task already. He'd let his curiosity and confusion get the best of him.

"No worries Mike. I'm on my way thanks for the heads up."

Michael looked around the office, then back at the computer screen. What was wrong? Gregory Wyman on the face of it seemed nothing more than a recluse. No matter how many times he looked at it all, he couldn't find what was going on. He'd seen a rape allegation levied against Mr Wyman back in 1976, made by a 16 year old girl. The case was dropped after the girl hung herself. She left a note stating all the allegations were in fact false.

What bothered Mike was the fact Wyman didn't, had never, and given his age of 59, probably would never have any children. The question kept on having to be asked. Why involve Jimmy and who was the missing girl?

Then it hit him! Could the rape case have been genuine? If it had been the girl in question may not have written the note and her hanging may not have been suicide! It was a stretch, but if Wyman was a paedophile, could his "Daughter" be the Priest's latest victim? Again, if that was the case, why involve Jimmy? Then confusion hit, did he inform someone, he'd been sharing this information with outside sources, should he call B.O.S 90? He didn't fully trust them, but if it meant catching the Priest would it not be worth it?

Chapter 12

Marcus Krueger sat at the table, of what he had to admit was a beautiful, and exclusive wine bar. He was beginning to worry. Marcus and Gregor had agreed to meet at 11.45, it was now 12.25, and Gregor was never late. Marcus was also becoming angry with his long term business partner, he had been sat here, for just shy of an hour, with a briefcase containing £81,000,000! He'd thrown in an extra million as he was hoping, Gregor could organise Marcus a rather special evening, with a girl he could do unspeakable things to. Now he was simply growing impatient.

Finally, Gregor Klichkov strolled into the wine bar. He was followed by a mountain of a man. At least Marcus was polite enough to call this monster, a man. This green mohawked, black suit, and tie wearing, punk rocker was easily 7ft 10", with a hulking muscular frame, he dwarfed Gregor by an easy 2ft. Marcus was drawn to the tattoos either side of his strip of hair. On the right side of this horror show's head, was adorned with an intricate spider web. The left depicted a Chinese dragon.

Gregor sat opposite Marcus, whilst the behemoth remained standing, behind Gregor. Marcus thought this beast was so tall where he stood, he could rest his bollocks atop of Gregor's balding head. He almost laughed at the image forming in his mind.

"So, what do you think of my new bodyguard?" Questioned Gregor.

"Very impressive specimen. Are you sure he can be trusted?" Marcus didn't like new people.

"He's been properly vetted." Klichkov assured him.

"I assume, you have the payment." Gregor continued. Marcus simply nodded and slid the briefcase across, now all he needed was to broach the request of a hotel room and girl, ideally out of the monster's earshot.

Chapter 13

After some bullshit about Christine's Mother being Caribbean, Wyman told me he had adopted Christine 8 years ago. I still didn't buy it, so I sent him to get me a copy of the adoption papers. Once he left the room, I removed the browning pistol from my waistband and flicked off the safety. I really didn't trust this fucker. I placed the gun in my pocket. It would be easier to get to if the situation did go off, and it might, because if he came back with anything other than adoption papers, he'd be eating bullets!

He entered the room, my arm tensed. He offered me the papers, I in turn discretely replaced the safety on my weapon. I flicked through what he'd given me. It appeared he was finally telling the truth, but why lie in the first place. My instincts were telling me to cap the twat. How was a man like this allowed to adopt in the first place?

I started again with a new line of questioning. First, I asked if there was any way Christine may have found her real parents, and run off, or if there was anyone with a grudge against him. He answered both with a flat no.

"How did you know my parents Mr Wyman?" I asked out of the blue, hoping to catch him off guard. It worked. Wyman looked almost shocked, looking at me then the door.

"Please I just want to know." I tried to get him to empathize with me. That didn't work.

"What relevance does that have to do with MY Christine?" He snapped, and he had me there, it had nothing to do with his "Daughter", but everything to do with why I was sat here. So, I decided to push on, hard if I had to.

"Humour me, or I could just ask the question I've had since I got here!" I had him. His eyes locked firmly on mine.

"And what would that be?" Asked Wyman, the knowledge of my parents unnerved him, almost more, it seemed than his daughter's disappearance. Why?

"Why did you lie about the police being involved?" Wyman fixed me with an icy stare.

"What do you mean? I didn't lie about the police!" He stated incredulously. I stared straight at him.

"Do I have to disprove everything you tell me?!" I was getting pissed off, talking to Wyman was like pulling teeth, and I decided to let him know. He looked angry, he glared at me, I stared back unmoved.

"O.K you don't want to tell me anything you don't have to. I'm sure you can find the girl yourself. Now I'd appreciate a name of someone who can help me!" I demanded.

I finally backed off, the combined smell of vodka, and body odour, was starting to make me feel really nauseous.

"Michelle Davies." Wyman said with little conviction.

"Who's that?" I enquired further, it wasn't a name I knew.

"She's your Aunt on your Father's side." Shit an Aunt, I couldn't believe it. Grandpa had never made any mention of any other family, other than Uncle Sonny. I had to get out of here.

"Right decision time. You want me to find the girl or not?" I put it bluntly, I couldn't start an investigation on the sort of answers he was giving to me.

"I think I'd rather you just left Mr Denim, I'll find someone else." He suddenly sounded defeated, as handed me an envelope filled with fifty pound notes. "I'm sorry to have wasted your time." He said, and with that I left.

As I walked down the road toward my car, I reached into my pocket, and fished out my phone as I scrolled through my contacts looking for Michael's number, I heard a man running up behind me.

"JIMMY!" It was Ali.

"What's up?" I asked him. He just stared at me for a few moments, before speaking.

"What did you find out?" He was completely out of breath.

"Walk and talk." I suggested. I wanted to get as far away from this Wyman prick as I could, as quickly as I could. I told him what had happened, which he said correlated with what Mike had found, although Mike hadn't mentioned anything about an adoption.

"I think this one's best handled by the police mate." Ali advised me.

"You may be right mate, but something tells me, even they won't find that poor little girl." I stated, still feeling the urge to not only find her myself but keep her well away from that piece of shit I'd just left!

We organised to meet Michael and Kate in a pub. Myself and Ali had pints of Stella in front of us, Michael and Kate, who were on duty, had J2Os. We sat discussing the results of this morning's findings. That's when Michael dropped the bombshell.

"I believe you've stumbled into an ongoing investigation, bro, one that's above our pay grade, apparently, it's definitely above yours." Michael told us. Kate took over.

"I think it's fair to say, his relationship with Christine is probably not as innocent as he's letting on." She summed it up quite politely. Ali not so much.

"HE'S A FUCKIN' NONCE!"

"Right, I think this case may be linked with the case we picked up yesterday." Mike stated.

"I'm sorry lads, but you're well and truly out of your depth with this one." He finished.

Out of my depth, cheeky fucker, I thought to myself. He was right, but fuck leaving this now, it was too big!

"You said you'd seen the adoption papers Jimmy." Kate invited me back in, I'd always liked Kate. I didn't know why Michael had never chanced his arm there.

"Yeah, they looked the real deal to me." I replied, fighting the urge to mention something about being out of my depth, but still trying to see where she was heading with this.

"What adoption agency is going to let a man like Wyman adopt a young girl?" Kate asked again. I thought back to the papers Wyman had shown me, what was the name of the Registrar on it? I knew what she was getting at now, she was beginning to think as I was, that Wyman was in league with a highly organised paedophile ring.

Caroline Partridge-Banks that was the Registrar on the paperwork, the one who had given Christine to Wyman. Michael decided that he and Kate would head over and speak with her. Before they left Mike pulled me to one side.

"Promise me you're off this now, I can't be having you two John Wayneing through this now." He stated.

"Yeah sure." I spoke.

"Finding kidnap victims is your job. I'm just security now, I get it." I assured him.

"Good, but whilst we are here, during your time in the Paras, did you ever hear of a group from MI5 called BOS90?" he asked, I stated I hadn't, and why, not understanding what that could have to do with the case.

"They came in to take over the case. Told me it was above my pay grade. I think they're ex-military, even though I recognised one of them." He informed me.

"I suppose it's possible, I mean these agencies do tend to hire ex-forces." I told my Brother.

"Yeah, I guess. I'm just not entirely convinced by them." He finished. We said our goodbyes, and Michael and Kate left.

Ali and I sat back down in one of the booths, at the far end of the pub, another couple of pints, and a review of our options. With a quarter of my pint left I prepared to neck it.

"I'm going to get down to my Aunt's, see what she can tell me about Wyman and my parents, and how we all fit in to this shit." I told Ali, he said it wasn't a bad shout, and that he'd head back to the office, and do some work on the accounts. With that we parted company for the day.

I found my Aunt's address quite quickly, it was on a small estate in Penge. Not one the nicest places I'd ever been, but a marked improvement on Wyman's hovel. There were two blocks of maisonette flats, in almost an L shape, with a car park and green that filled up the rest of the estate. I knocked loudly three times, the door was answered by a woman in her fifty's. She looked shocked, as she looked at me, like I was a ghost, and had just walked through the door to greet her.

"Mrs Davies?" I said more as a question, but also letting on I knew exactly who she was.

"That's me." She confirmed cautiously. I knew now she was aware I was her Nephew, but not sure which one.

"Jimmy." I said offering my hand, she ignored it. Her eyes filling with tears, she grabbed me, and hugged me crying into my chest.

I looked at my Aunt. She was short with grey hair, her skin was pale. I knew she was a junkie instantly. Once she'd regained her composure, she invited me in. I stepped into the hallway, there were stairs at the end on the left hand side, to my immediate left was a small kitchen, dirty plates from the night before sat on the draining board. Also, at the end of the hallway just after the stairs, was a small living room. Michelle led me down to it. There were two sofas both cream on a burgundy carpet. Central to the room was a small coffee table, on it sat an ashtray.

"Aunt Michelle. I need to ask you a few questions." I stated as we sat on opposing sofas.

"Oh, and what are they?" My enquired. I lit a smoke without thinking, Michelle didn't complain simply passing me the ashtray.

"I'm sorry to ask, but do you know what happened to my parents?" I asked.

"Well, they were shot duck." Was my Aunt's direct response. I stopped to think for a moment, taking a long drag on my cigarette.

"Michelle, do you have any pictures of them I could have? I've never seen any." She looked upset by this, and headed upstairs, saying she'd be just a few seconds.

She returned down with a picture of two men, both in expensive suits. I took another long drag on my cigarette, as she pointed to the fella, on the right of the picture. I knew what she was going to say instantly.

"That's your Dad." Like I said instantly, he looked just like me, albeit without hair and a few different scars. I stubbed out my smoke. I motioned my pack in offer of a fresh cigarette for my Aunt.

"Who's the other guy?" I asked, as she took the smoke. Her response came as she lit it, and I sparked another up myself.

"That's Ray. We had a bit of a thing in eighties, after his wife died. He was the one who took over your Dad's bars." I asked how that had worked. That's when she told me, my Dad had been a gangster with a string of small business', along with my Grandfather, Uncle Santino, and Ray had been my father's right hand man.

"Do you think, this Ray could've shot my parents?" I asked.

"Dear god no!" She screamed seemingly shocked I could possibly think such a thing. Then she told me it was a professional job. Apparently well out of my Dad, and Ray's league.

"The shooter was so good your father was lucky to get a shot off, apparently."

I was sent reeling, by the knowledge of how my parents had been dispatched. If I hadn't been just 6 months old at the time, it could almost have been me that killed them.

"Have you any idea why they were killed?" I had to ask, it could've pointed the finger at someone.

"Your Father knew something, it worried him. Your Father was very troubled the last time I saw him alive, that's when he signed the bars over to Ray." I had to see this Ray if he was still around. I asked if he was and where I could find him.

"Oh, Ray's still around." Michelle laughed, I noticed there was more affection in her voice with every mention of this man's name.

"He's still got your Dad's old pub down the bottom of Hawthorn." She told me. We sat catching up for another hour or two, then I gave her my phone number and said goodbye.

Chapter 14

Krueger walked into his warehouse. There were approximately 300 migrant worker's scurrying round, loading pallets. Two polish men were outside the large vehicle door, guiding in a reversing delivery van, an hour after it was due, he might add. He allowed himself a small smile knowing this would be his "art" delivery, fresh from the Klichkov gallery.

The operation was simple the "art" was delivered to the warehouse, the drugs would be harvested, and the art then delivered to various brothels. The drugs would also be delivered to a few selected dealers, who would distribute the product down to local gangs, some of which had family working in this very warehouse. He called over four Iraqi men, to remove the paintings from the truck. In just a matter of hours Krueger would be counting his profits and punishing some young whore!

That was what he had thought anyway, 5 hours later and Krueger was still pacing up and down his office. A job which should have been completed in 3 hours had taken 5. Things had been moving far too slowly for his liking. he would punish someone for that! A young Vietnamese girl burst into his office her face full of excitement. She told him the paintings were finally loaded. Finally, Krueger knew this meant the drugs would also be separated, and ready to be distributed to the smaller suppliers.

He headed down to the worker's area. Before him stood some 300 migrant workers. All in this country illegally, by his hand. However now a lesson had to be taught.

Krueger smiled as his eyes locked upon a small group of Kosovans, a man and woman may be in their fifties. Stood behind a man and woman in their twenties. The choice was made.

"You, come here!" Krueger demanded in harsh German tones. The 23 year old Kosovan boy obeyed, whilst his bemused family watched on. As the young man drew ever closer, he felt the heavy foreboding emanating, from his employer. Krueger smiled as the young man reached him. Without warning Krueger smashed his right hand into the young man's face. This attack dropping the lad, flat on his back.

As soon as the poor boy had landed Krueger was upon him. Krueger's smile had twisted into a wild grin, as he pulled a cosh from his waistband. Without hesitation Marcus renewed his attack, slamming the cosh into his employee's kneecaps. The young man's Father rushed towards Krueger, leaving his wife and Daughter, crying in the crowd.

Krueger spotted the older migrant, running in to defend his child, but Marcus was as quick as he was ruthless. Instantly he pulled a colt revolver, from inside his jacket.

The Father froze, as Krueger's eyes narrowed, then two shots rang out. The man fell, Kruger looked down at the man's son, moving his gun down towards the boy, and he fired off five rounds into the lad's chest.

It made him feel good, but not as good as he would feel after this evenings activities. After all of today's aggravations he definitely needed to indulge himself, and his darkest desires!

Chapter 15

The next day I got to the office before Ali. Michael and Kate were waiting outside for us.

"Oh, this looks ominous. What can I do you pair for?" Michael wasn't looking amused, or happy. He explained there had been a major development in the Wyman case the prior evening.

"Some of our colleagues, are going to want to talk to you about it." Kate informed me, looking at me with an unusual sternness.

"Hang on, what the fucks going on?" I asked, they told me. I wish they fucking hadn't.

I'd been in the office an hour when Ali got in. I looked at him.

"What's wrong mate?" he asked. He must of seen the concern and pain in my face.

"The girls turned up. She's back with Wyman." I felt the tears welling up.

"What's going on Jim? How did Mike and Kate let that happen?" Ali asked, the answer unfortunately was quite horrific.

"There was a major development last night." I started to choke, trying to hold back how truly distressed the whole mess had made me.

"Firstly, the adoption papers were forged. Wyman was as we suspected a paedophile!" I was struggling to continue.

"What's happened?" Ali saw the torment I was suffering.

"They're both dead. Murdered. Cut about a hundred times, with a razor. Arms, legs, torso and face covered in tiny cuts. Then both had a crucifix carved into their throats!" I'd pretty much finished I let my fifth cigarette of the hour.

"Fuckin' hell mate! Who could do something like that to a 12 year old girl? I mean the nonce yeah fine, but the girl?" Ali like myself was struggling to make any sense to what was going on.

"He calls himself the Priest. According to BOS90, some MI5 offshoot. They say he leaves a calling card. He's killed before. Always kids already victims of paedophilia, and then their abusers." I had finished.

"Jesus. Why the victims and not just the paedophiles?" Ali continued to quiz me.

"No idea mates. Apparently, he's recently changed his M.O, to extorting money out of parents, but with Christine we think he's definitely operating under his old rules." I was going to catch him too, and when I did, he'd feel real fucking justice, the sick fuck! On top of this I still had to meet this Ray Valentine, even more so now to find out how my parents had known a dirty fucking paedophile cunt!

Chapter 16

It was pissing hard with rain as I walked down Hawthorne Grove, towards The Occasional Half. I lit a cigarette as I walked through the door. The pub had a nice atmosphere, a proper London boozer. Four tables were sat over one side of the pub, with the bar standing proud opposite the door. A pool table occupied the other side. There was a couple playing. The girl was a very beautiful brunette, when I looked at the guy she was with, well I thought she could've done a lot better. It was quite busy for a weekday afternoon, with three of the four tables being occupied by different groups.

There were two large blokes laden in gold and tattoos, both in their fifties. Then a table of teenagers, some clearly over 18 others clearly not. There was a fat, poorly dressed middle aged mess at the other, who got up and climbed onto a barstool. In front of him was a bored looking barmaid. I sat down the bar from the obvious regular. I spied him paying for his latest pint with shrapnel. Then I let my eyes cast over the barmaid, and what she wasn't wearing. She was stunning. I'd have put her at 20/22. Her curly blonde hair cascaded down to her shoulders. I was drawn to her deep soulful brown eyes. She had an air of confidence about her as she sauntered down the walkway behind the bar. She was dressed in a short skirt, and halter neck top that showed off her toned midriff.

"What can I get ya soldier?" Asked the angel behind the bar.

"Uh pint of Stella cheers love. Is it that obvious I was in the army?" I asked a little shocked.

"You're kidding right? You've got military tattooed on your forehead." She said with a chuckle.

"Oh, and what's your view on squaddies then?"

"They're alright for a laugh but that's it. Why did you wanna try and chat me up?" She asked handing my pint over the bar, whilst leaning just enough to show off her cleavage.

"What you? Nah barmaids are alright for a laugh but that's about it." I replied flashing my cheekiest grin, she laughed.

"That'll be £2.90 then action man." She informed me, I sipped at my pint, then allowed my stare to pass the gorgeous creature before me, behind the bar I spotted an older man walking around the back room, and I shit you not it was fucking Frank Sinatra! Alright it wasn't really but he was the spit of old blue eyes, and the man I had come here to see.

I drained my lager, eager to speak to Ray. However not eager enough not to order another pint. Then I felt a hand on my shoulder.

"You got any bugle boi?" I turned it was the lad from the pool table. His hair was greasy, and his breath stank.

"No, I ain't!" I told him bluntly.

"Ya wants some?" I looked him up, and down before telling him.

"Fuck off lad." He walked off muttering to himself. I sank my new beer, indicating my empty glass to the goddess.

"Fuckin' hell, you're knocking them back, got a thirst on, have we?" She chuckled.

"No point wasting time is there? Grab one for yourself as well this time." I told her.

"Thanks." She replied, just as two lads walked in. Both looked as shifty as arseholes. They had baseball caps on with their heads down. One was fiddling with something in his jacket. At first, I discounted them as kids trying to get served, as had the barmaid.

"Two Fosters please darlin'." Asked the most confident of the shifty pair.

"Got any I.D?" Came the response from the golden haired beauty, who clearly thought the same as me. Then I saw it. Jutting out the bottom of his jacket, was the barrel of a shotgun, but it was too late! He lifted it so it was now placed directly under the barmaid's chin.

"No, but will this do?" I flinched as he said this, and his mate was on me. He waved a Smith and Wesson in my face.

"No heroics pal!" I was informed coldly.

"Everyone on the ground now!" Yelled the shotgun totting scroat, we all complied for now.

"Put ya valuables in front of ya, and you treacle can empty the till into this bag!" He produced a small sports bag forcing it into her hands. I watched as the toe rag with the hand gun walked around the pub. I looked up towards the dickhead with the shotgun, his attention fully on the barmaid.

My hand shot up and I gripped his bollocks, using them to pull myself up. He yelped and spun the shotgun in my direction. Unfortunately for him, I was now behind him. I grabbed the barrel dragging it alongside me, as I head-butted him. He let go of the weapon, and I swung it like a baseball bat, slamming the butt into the underside of his jaw.

His mate turned to see what was going on. He was too late as well. I already had the shotgun trained on him.

"Drop it now!" I instructed him. He did instantly.

"Now get over here!" He walked slowly toward me. I spun the shotgun in my hands, with a short sharp twist of my waist, I caught him almost identically to his mate.

"Jesus fuckin' H Christ! What were you S.A.S?" The barmaid finally spoke.

"Nah 2 Para. So anyway, do you got a name, or do I call you barmaid, during the police interview?" I asked.

"It's Carly Jane, C.J for short, and if I didn't know better, I'd say you were trying to chat me up again." She replied.

"Well, it's a good thing you know better." I Laughed.

I turned as I got a sudden waft of B.O, I knew it wasn't Carly. It was the regular.

"You leave her alone pal!" He slurred, his expression one of pure hatred, even after what I had done.

"Sorry mush, firstly I don't know you, secondly can I get these two fuck wits dealt with, before contending with your stench!?" I produced a pair of zip ties, from my inside jacket pocket, the regular huffed and walked over to the other side of the bar. Whilst I propped to unconscious pair of shit bags up against the bar, securing their hands together back to back. I saw Carly pick up the phone and call the police.

Chapter 17

Judge Martin Hollinson had taken his Daughter Sophie to the local park. It was a beautiful day. Sophie was 8 years old, and Martin watched as the sunlight danced on her long blonde hair. Her brown eyes always full of mischief.

They had done everything that day. The slide, the swings and now Sophie was running amok with the other kids on the climbing frame. Then she ducked into the tunnel, Martin waited for her to shoot out the other side.

She didn't. He waited five minutes before walking over there.

"Sophie, come on honey time to go now. "Martin called out to her. He poked his head around to look through the tunnel. It was empty. His stomach wrenched, his head started swimming, and he was sweating profusely. Fear swept over him in waves. How did this happen?

Martin searched everywhere for her. It took him 20 minutes to cover the entirety of the park, to no avail. He took out his mobile and called the police. He stood waiting at the park entrance, waiting for the police to arrive. It felt like an eternity, as he struggled to wait, pacing up and down. Then out of nowhere, he heard Sophie call him. He turned round and there she was. A wave of relief hit him.

"The man said to give you this Daddy." She said handing her Father a note.

Judge Hollinson

Your Daughter Sophie has been with us for the last hour. If you don't want to lose her again you will pay us £50,000 and have P.C Chris Fitzgerald, make the drop! If these instructions are not adhered to, you will never see your Daughter again. We hope we make ourselves clear. We will contact you with the time and location!

It was another 5 minutes before two police officers arrived. Hollinson picked his Daughter up in his arms, terrified of letting her go again, and headed over to the two officers. One appeared to be in his mid-40's, bald with a big bushy beard, the other looked fresh out of college early 20's clean shaven with a blonde French crop.

"Mr Hollinson, I'm P.C Forrest, this is my colleague P.C Riley." Declared the older officer. Hollinson swallowed hard and explained to both officers what had transpired over the last hour, before handing over the note. The officers then requested, Hollinson and his Daughter, go to the station with them, making it sound like a grand outing to Sophie, Martin knew better but agreed and accompanied them back to their car.

Chapter 18

Ray had come through, from the back room. He clearly wanted to know what was going on in his pub. There had been a flash of recognition in his eyes when he'd seen me. To start with I thought, maybe he'd met Michael.

He refused to acknowledge me, until after the police had been, and completed their interviews, followed by the subsequent arrests, and left. In that time, a young lad entered the pub, he was early20's, with dark medium length swept back hair. The rest of his appearance was a bit scruffy. It turned out he was a barman, so once he had arrived Ray approached me.

"What's your surname boy?" He asked, his voice steeped in anger, no thank you for saving my staff and money, or customers, or kiss my arse nothing.

"Denim! And I ain't no fucking boy! I'm a grown man thanks, you old cunt!" He'd pissed me off and I decided to let him know just how much.

"I'm sorry, It's just you look so much like him, but I still had to be sure." Ray stated apologetically.

"You'd best come through, to the back." He added, so I followed him through.

As we headed through the door, at the back of the bar. Ray stopped.

"So, is it Michael or James?" He asked.

"Actually, it's Jimmy." I replied.

As we walked through to Ray's living area, I was impressed at how clean and tidy it was. Then I was stopped, as we walked into the living room. On the wall directly opposite me, was 20 maybe 30, framed photographs surrounding a plague. The inscription read: -

Barry Denim 19/3/1931 – 11/12/1978

Tina Denim 18/7/1937 – 11/12/1978

Better people we've never known

May they rest in peace.

"Sit down lad, I think this is a chat to be had over a bottle." As he spoke, I kept half expecting him to break into "My Way" So I sat and watched as he brought out a bottle of jack to the table.

"You were going to tell me about my parents." I stated as Ray sat opposite me, and solemnly poured two glasses of jack.

"Yeah, I was. Forgive me as I don't know everything you'll want to know. I only have what your Father told me."

"I'd like to start by saying, the shrine you've got there it's a bit much. Isn't it?" I half stated, knocking back my whisky, it's burn strangely comforting. Ray poured me another, whilst nursing his own.

"Not for me thanks I'm driving." I told him knowing I was already well over the limit.

"Then you'll stay here. As for the memorial, your Father wasn't just my business partner he was my closest friend." The pain clearly still evident in his voice.

I eventually agreed, to stay, although I wasn't sure it was the right choice, I'd only just met these people and not many people even knew I was here, Ray could've been anyone. As Ray told me the story, as he knew it, I used the alcohol to mask my pain, as I had more than developed a knack for over the last few years. With that I made a conscious effort to call both Ali, and then Liz, letting them know where I was and what was happening. I promised to keep them both posted on any developments. Finally making sure Liz knew to contact Michael, if she had any more problems with Warren.

As I re-joined Ray in the back room, Carly brushed passed me.

"Would you like a cuppa Jimmy?" She asked, I told her I was fine, as I was more than happy with the whisky. I watched as she walked past Ray, and into the adjoining kitchen. The back room was quite small and like a living room/diner. There was a sofa leaning against the wall with a TV opposite, they were to the right of the doorway. In between the door I stood in, and the entrance to the kitchen was an oak dining table and chairs. This is where Ray was sat. He had a similar air to Paulie about him, albeit a tad elder school.

As Ray and me, continued our conversation I found my attention continuously drawn to Carly in the kitchen. Her eyes had been trained on me, for the entirety of my visit.

"She's beautiful, isn't she?" Ray asked knowing the answer.

"Sure is." I agreed without looking back at Ray and taking a large gulp of whisky.

"There's just one problem with her." He added slowly, in a matter of fact way.

"Yeah, what's that?" I asked, instantly wishing I hadn't, as I heard Ray's answer.

"She's, my Daughter." He informed me, his face now an intimidating glare. That's when I finally saw the once revered south east London gangster.

"Jimmy, you didn't come here to eye up my Daughter. So, what do you want to know?" Ray asked sternly, I was getting the impression he was beginning to dislike me, but then his Daughter and I had been giving each other the fucking googly eyes. Hell, I'd have the same reaction if some fucking upstart came to my house and was doing the same thing with Lacey! It was either that or my presence and questions were scaring him. If he was scared, he was hiding it well. His new found abrasiveness just made me surer he knew something.

"I know my parents were killed over something my Father knew." I stated. "And I want to know what it was he found out. If I know that I can find who killed them." I finished, Ray's face dropped, a fear, real fucking fear entered his eyes.

"How much did Michelle tell you?" Was all he offered in response.

"As much as she could, I think. Definitely enough to know you weren't involved, but you do know more than she does!" I responded, I'd seen the fear in his eyes now was the time to push.

"Carly, babe could you make yourself scarce." Ray commanded as if he were asking.

"O.K Daddy." Definite Daddy's girl. We sat for a while as Carly made her way upstairs.

"This is delicate Jimmy. I'm risking everything just letting you in the door." After that announcement, I felt obligated to allow Ray to go out to the bar and grab us some more whisky. It sounded like we were going to need it!

I lit a cigarette the whole time wondering, what was this big bad gangster so fucking scared of? Then I heard a female scream from upstairs, it had to be Carly! I pulled my Gloch from my waistband attaching the silencer. I rounded the door checking the hallway was clear. Slowly I made my way down the corridor to the stairs. I slowly climbed the steps again slowly trying to mask my footfalls. There were multiple doors upstairs, but to her credit Carly wasn't giving up without a fight her screams filled the immediate vicinity, allowing me to find the room.

As I burst through the door, gun first. I will never forget what I saw, or how it made me feel!

There on the bed was Carly. She was being held by a balding middle aged man. I saw her underwear, a pink thong yanked down to her ankles. Her assailant had a large hunting knife resting heavily on her throat. He was clearly attempting to rape her, fortunately he hadn't entered her yet! I felt both disgusted and increasingly pissed off! Instinctively I fired off three rounds. The first skimmed her attacker's shoulder. In a shocked panic he rolled of the bed. The other two shots had been hopelessly off target, the second shot had hit the window, as the third had embedded itself in the wall.

Maybe I'm not as good a shot, as I thought I was. Then I saw the bastard! Appearing over the bed again. I fired again the round skimming his head as he ducked. Missed again, but at least it brought me time to drag, a now sobbing Carly out of the way. Then I saw him, through a clear mask, grinning at me! He rushed at us, fast! Instinctively I pushed Carly away and tried to use the momentum of my shove to get myself clear of his knife. I was milliseconds too slow and felt the edge of his blade slide across my chest.

I heard him slam into the wall, turn and start up the hall. I turned to get after him, but Carly grabbed my arm.

"Don't leave me, please." She begged. There was no sign of the confident young woman I'd met earlier.

After a short while, I took her downstairs to the bar. It was empty, except for Ray. He was sat in the corner, he looked at me then Carly.

"I'm sorry honey, there was nothing I could do." He said solemnly tears filling his blue eyes.

"I know Dad." She stammered through tears of her own.

"I think we all need a good fucking drink and a chat, don't you?" I stated as Ray managed a nod in agreement.

Chapter 19

Marcus paced up and down in his office. He stopped as his phone rang, answering it on the fourth ring.

"Hello is it done?" He questioned the caller. Marcus became visibly more agitated by the response.

"This young man is becoming a seriously irritating problem!" He continued.

"P.C Fitzgerald, is our most pressing concern for now, the Denim boy will have to wait for now." As he paused, the caller's response again caused Krueger's blood to boil! This time he allowed his anger to spill out, as he kicked his computer off his oak desk.

"Your liberty or incarceration ARE NOT MY FUCKING CONCERN! You do as you're told, or you die! IT'S THAT FUCKING SIMPLE!" Marcus Krueger had thought he had made his feelings on failure clear, to all in his employ. This phone call however, had suggested his most prized employee, was in need of a swift reminder.

Marcus had ended the call, by giving the Priest, a further berating, before calling Klichkov, for a bollocking of his own. The Priest's days could well be numbered, if he failed again, a sentiment made abundantly clear, by a very perturbed Klichkov. This saddened Krueger, but he coldly agreed as he knew, a man like the Priest was far too dangerous, to fall into the hands of the authorities.

Chapter 20

It had been hours, since Judge Hollinson, had received the ransom note. He'd sat in the police station all day, and still hadn't received the call, from the kidnappers. Then a P.C in his mid, to late twenties entered the room. He was tall and broad, the Judge would put him at 6ft 3". He wore Blonde cropped hair, and tattoos down both forearms clearly on show. The young copper carried himself with an air of immense confidence, which bordered on arrogance.

"Judge Hollinson?" Enquired the P.C, Hollinson simply nodded in acknowledgement, all his energy sapped from the stress of the day.

"I'm P.C Chris Fitzgerald, I understand what's happened. I do however have a few questions."

It turns out this Fitzgerald fella, had received the call from the kidnappers. He'd proceeded to fire his questions at Hollinson. Who had done his best too answer, unfortunately without knowing the identity of the kidnappers, he couldn't answer his or the young P. C's most burning question? Why P.C Fitzgerald? The young P.C, had to his credit stepped up and agreed to comply with the kidnapper's demands.

"There are a few more officers, who would like to speak to you Judge." Fitzgerald advised. Hollinson was getting agitated now. This was exactly what was wrong with the law in this country, everything moved so fucking slowly! It was then that D.C Marshall poked her head around the door. P.C Fitzgerald gave her a nod, as she entered, three other plainclothes officers' two males and another female followed her in. One of the male officers looked furious, and he was it was Michael.

Michael had been seriously pissed off, from the moment Agents Fuller, and Daniels had turned up at the initial crime scene. For all their posturing, at the cinema and Wyman's place, these MI5 "super cops" had offered very little help in identifying this Priest character. Now Agent Daniels had hatched some half-baked, bullshit op to use Hollinson, P.C Fitzgerald and fifty grand as bait. Michael knew something was wrong, he just couldn't work out what.

Chapter 21

Three hours and three bottles of wine later, we returned to the whisky. Ray had already explained why he'd been so useless. The 20 something barman, Stewart as I had been informed, had ordered everyone out of the pub, whilst we'd been in the backroom. Then when Ray had gone in to grab us the whisky, Stewart had put a gun to Ray's head, informing him, his boss wanted Ray to know what was happening to his little girl.

"Shame, if they'd asked me, I'd have done her for free!" The scroat had told Ray. When Ray had told us that part, I felt my anger rising again. I was beginning to feel increasingly intoxicated, by the alcohol, and Carly. This was a bad situation, for the last three hours she hadn't taken her eyes off me. Maybe it had something to do with me having saved her life twice in the first 12 hours of meeting her.

After another bottle of whisky, started doing the rounds, I was feeling seriously pissed, but still had enough about me to listen to what Ray was telling me, just. Apparently, my Father had signed everything over to Ray, just days before he was murdered. Ray was to hold the businesses for my Mother or Michael and me. This was allegedly because my Father, had inadvertently gotten involved with some real hardnosed bastards, with contacts all over the place. These fuckers had some very dirty fingers, in every grubby little pie. Ray was very clear these people scared the shit out him, they were into drugs, robberies, gun-running all the up to people trafficking, and murder. Worst of all was the power they wielded, using that power to control and cover up paedophile rings.

It was the first time I really contemplated how big a part Wyman may have had in, what had happened to my parents. It was also starting to dawn on me, these people maybe too big to take down legally. The police and justice system hadn't caught up with them in over 30 years, what chance did they have now? I also started to think, could the Priest be involved with the organisation? If he, was it could have been him upstairs with C.J.?

I felt sick my head spun at the thought, I'd either survived a run-in with the Priest, or failed to kill him! Next time he wouldn't be so fucking lucky! The theory of the Priest somehow being connected to this criminal super power, just made sense, I thought. It would give him access to his victims and they're abductions, but I wanted proof of this, until then I couldn't be 100% sure.

Then Ray gave me Stewart's address.

"I want that little cunt dead Jim!" Ray said, I tried to tell him I ran a security firm, I was some mafia hit man.

"So why do you carry a silenced pistol?" Ray asked. Shit how'd he knows about that?

"Jimmy I've heard everything about you. I've not lost all my contacts, and I'm not likely too with Paulie Shawcross still drawing breathe!"

What!? Paulie knew Ray? But that would've meant Paulie knew my Dad, and never mentioned it.

"I hear you're very good." Ray stated. Nausea enveloped me.

"If you knew who I was, where I was, and who I was with, why didn't you find me?" I asked, that's when Ray hit me with an icy stare and the brick wall revelation.

"I did, me and Paul decided to watch over you. Paul owns all your old man's businesses, other than this one. Paul was in a better position to protect you. And prepare you to take charge of the Denim Empire, I mean you're a decent soldier by all accounts but your no gangster."

The Denim Empire? This was getting ridiculous! It's true me and Michael were no angels growing up, but the sons of some big time gangster?

"How do you know Paulie then?" I asked, the account I was hearing just sent my brain into overdrive.

"He was part of your old man's firm. Like me. Unlike me he was a complete head case." He informed me.

"My old man's firm it just sounds ridiculous." I couldn't wrap my head round it.

"If you guys were such big time gangsters how comes none of you know, or have dealt with the people responsible for killing my parents?" I pushed after all the fucking shitty jobs I'd done for Paulie, and that cunt was running round on my old man's fucking coat tails all these years! I was fucking raging!

"We were fucking big time, for London. The guys you're dealing with now Jim, there fucking international!" His head dropped again like I'd hit a nerve. C.J jumped to her Father's rescue.

"I think that's enough for tonight. Jimmy, you look exhausted." She told me. "Go get some sleep you can use my room." She added.

"That's alright sweetheart I'll be fine on the sofa." I responded.

"One more for the road?" Ray offered, hovering the bottle of jack over my glass.

"Yeah, one won't hurt. Cheers Ray."

As I drank the last mouthful, Ray fixed me with another of his hard stares.

"I meant what I said earlier about Stewart! I want him dead Jimmy, and I'll pay you to do it." I stood there for a moment, holding Ray's stare with one of my own.

"I'm glad you asked I'll do him for free!" I replied and headed for his sofa before he could respond.

I didn't sleep well that night. Staying at Ray's was uncomfortable, he seemed honest enough, but I was becoming very untrusting of the people around me. It had dawned on me I hadn't spoken to Paulie in four days, meaning tomorrow my week was almost up he'd be sending someone to pay us a visit, for the £13,000 he thought I owed him. He'd be lucky, after what I'd just learnt, I'll be taking him for everything his got!

Chapter 22

Michael and Kate sat in the unmarked Vauxhall Astra, they'd been issued, looking out into the dark.

"This OP is absolute Bollocks!" Exclaimed Michael finally, Kate gave him an acknowledging look of concern.

"I know Mike but what can we do?" She asked. The deeper into this case they became, the clearer it was to Michael, these kidnappers were incredibly efficient, organised, and professional. All the qualities you don't want in your criminal gangs! Because these qualities made them almost impossible to catch, and if you did catch them, it was almost guaranteed they'd also have some hot shot lawyer. This hot shot would have them out, and reoffending within days if not hours, because to catch people like this you almost certainly needed to bend the rules, or ultimately ignore them altogether. That's why they were all sat here, at the entrance to Hampstead Heath, in the middle of the night!

The lack of light made it almost impossible to keep a clear view of Fitzgerald and the money. It was infuriating to Michael, who now suspected Fitzgerald of somehow being involved. Why else would a gang of kidnappers request a specific police officer, to perform a fifty grand drop? If he wasn't involved or compromised in some way none of this made any sense. Why have Hollinson share information with the police? Hollinson himself had insisted on being present, Michael understood that at least. However, he did feel a bit insulted when the Judge had chosen the two MI5 agents as his escort, over the two Met detectives. So there the Judge was sat in the back of Agent Fuller's Jaguar XF, another thing the Agents were happy to point out as "above your pay grade".

Then it happened. Fitzgerald vanished from view. Michael and Kate sprung from the car, sprinting to Fitzgerald's last known location, as did the two Agents. Fuck this was exactly what Michael had been worried about! The shit had hit the fan! As the four officers drew nearer to the P. C's position, the clearer it became to Michael.

"We've been set up!" He thought out loud. As P.C Fitzgerald's lifeless corpse came into view. Michael looked at Kate, who see the pain and disbelief in his eyes, as she fixed him with a similar expression.

"BOLLOCKS! HOLLINSON!" Screamed Agent Daniels, as she turned on a sixpence and raced back towards the car, pulling free her Government Issue handgun. Michael continued towards Fitzgerald. Dropping to his knees, and trying to obtain some sign of life, but they were too late. The young P.C was gone.

"Fuck, FULLER HELP ME!" Screamed Agent Daniels from the MI5 car. Fuller ran to his colleague, releasing his own firearm from its holster. Michael didn't move somehow, he already knew their failure was complete. He knew when they made their way back to the cars, they would not only find Judge Hollinson in that car, but his Daughter as well. Michael also knew they would both be dead. He couldn't face it, so he knelt in the dirt with Kate, and Fitzgerald's lifeless body, and cursed.

Chapter 23

In the morning I prepared to leave by 06:00, not being sure when Ray would be up to open the pub. I wasn't waiting long, as Carly sauntered in wearing a low cut pink silk dressing gown, which didn't leave much to the imagination. I was fucking mesmerised as the gown barely covered her pert arse.

"Morning my gorgeous hero." She said cheerily, in fact a little too cheerily for me, at six o'clock in the morning. Especially with what had transpired last night.

"Morning." Was all I could manage in response.

A few minutes later Ray walked in, in what honestly looked like the same outfit as the previous day. He fixed Carly with a hard stare.

"Jesus Carly! How many times cover yourself up!" It sounded to me as though it could be in the millions.

"Yes Daddy." She said giggling to herself as she ran upstairs.

I pulled out my Gloch and saw the shock on Ray's face.

"Sorry Ray just giving it a quick once over." I assured him.

"Thank fuck for that! I thought I'd upset you for a second there." He said with a chuckle.

"Do you know who Stewart's working for? I mean obviously they know you." I asked.

"No, I mean I assume it's to do with you and your parents." He answered, I knew there was more, but the more I thought about it the guiltier I felt. As I knew he was right.

"The last time something like this happened was in '79 when I tried finding out more for myself." Ray finally added confirming my guilt.

Fuck I'd led these bastards straight to Ray and Carly. I knew the mother fuckers didn't want to be found, it now seemed they knew I was looking for them. I was sure Stewart had notified them, of my presence in the pub yesterday, or maybe they'd been tipped off by Wyman. Whoever had alerted them, one thing was certain, I had to get to Stewart before they did!

"Ray Thanks for your hospitality, but I've got to go." I said replacing my gun back in my waistband.

"Okay lad, you go do what you've gotta do, just do me one more favour. Come back here, so we can sort you an alibi." I accepted, we exchanged numbers and I left.

It only took half an hour to find Stewart's address, fortunately there was a café on the corner of his road. I ran in grabbing a bacon roll, and a coffee to takeaway. Then came the wait. So, I sat in my car for another hour and a half, waiting for someone to leave the block of flats. They were rough and looked like a drugs den. Then a young lad came down the stairs, looking to exit the building. I jumped from the car, jogging over to reach the door, as this young lad made his exit. Once inside I checked my

Gloch and attached the silencer. I didn't want to wake the neighbours now, did I?

I started up the stairs, on my search for Stewart's flat. Just like in my block the aroma of piss filled the air. Thankfully Stewart's flat was only on the second floor. It occurred then as I stood outside my quarry's door, I'd rather rushed into this. I hadn't given myself a chance at any recon. I had no real plan either, other than to shoot him. I decided my best option was the brazen approach. I knocked on the door authoritatively, it was answered quickly by a young girl, with mousy blonde hair. She was wearing a large AC/DC shirt, like a night dress. I hated these new age kids, trying so hard to be retro. It was just embarrassing.

"Hi is Stewart about love?" I asked brushing past her, not waiting for an answer.

"It's alright, he should be expecting me." I informed her, well at least he would've if knew anything about me.

"And just who are you?" She finally asked incredulously, I paused and turned slowly. Staring her straight in the eyes.

"My name is Shawcross, and as I said he's expecting me!" I scowled as I gave Paulie's name, knowing if either had heard his name before it would get me immediate results. Also, I couldn't give her my real name considering this girl may be about to witness a murder.

"I'm so sorry Mr. Shawcross, I assumed you'd be older." I stopped that had caught me of guard. That sounded almost as if Stewart was expecting Paulie! Was Stewart working for Paulie?

I turned to the young girl, her hair unwashed and unkempt, her eyes red and looking sore.

"Why don't you go put the kettle on love?" I asked wanting her out the way, then opportunity knocked.

"We ain't got no milk." I took my chance. The girl was clearly a junkie, but I could do without a witness, so it was get rid of her, or kill her. I pulled a £20 from my wallet and handed it to her.

"Tell ya what then, why don't you run down the shops and get some?" I suggested, thinking this would give me ten minutes if she actually went to get milk, to well over an hour if she went to score. As she yanked the cash from my hand and ran out the door, I knew what her choice was.

"Who is it Rach?" A male voice called from the living room. I walked in, gun outstretched in front of me, taking in my surroundings. I caught the strong smell of marijuana. It was no wonder as I spotted a fish tank in the corner filled with the stuff. The place was full of drugs and their paraphernalia. Stewart was running a drugs factory.

I spotted him sitting on a chair in the corner of the room. My gun trained on him instantly. I felt the smile spread across my face, as I watched the fear wash over his.

"Hello Stewart, who are you working for?" I asked in a playfully sinister tone. Stewart chuckled.

"You don't know?" He derived, but not for long. I pulled the trigger, and the bullet slammed into his left kneecap. He let out a blood curdling scream, reaching for his own gun tucked in the back of his jeans. Fucking amateurs I thought. I was on top of him in seconds the barrel of my Gloch now resting on his temple. I took special care to rest my right boot on his disintegrating kneecap and snatched his gun away.

I asked again.

"Who are you working for Stewart? Is it Paul? Is it Paulie Shawcross?" He nodded, as tears streamed down his face.

"So, Paulie gave the order yesterday?" I asked, Stewart stared at me defiantly.

"I do hope you weren't hoping for a career playing football Stewart." I informed him, as I fired another round into his right knee this time.

"How gave the FUCKING ORDER STEWART?!" I placed the barrel on his crutch.

"I won't ask again!" I stated, allowing my anger to turn my words into a snarl.

"It wasn't Paulie! I sell drugs for him that's all! Yesterday came from above Paul's head!" I'd found his button he was singing like a canary now.

"Who gave me up then? Was it Paulie or Wyman?" I needed to know if Paulie was involved in any way.

"It was the copper! The one that interviewed you!" He was panicking and making too much noise, but I needed more!

"P.C Fitzgerald?" I asked.

"Yeah, that's him! He works for my other boss who runs the security on Ray and keeps an eye on all of you!" What the fuck was going on?

"Who's keeping an eye on who?" I asked pushing down on my gun.

"John! John O'Grady!" He screamed.

"The Paddy that runs the club over on George Street?" I asked again. This really wasn't making any sense. John O'Grady wasn't a gangster, and even if he was, he was nowhere near Shawcross' level.

"Yeah, he keeps an eye on all you Denim lot!" I decided that was enough for now. I was running out of time, the junkie whore would be back shortly, if, (and I very much doubted It.) she had gone for milk, and not to buy drugs.

I lifted my gun to his forehead.

"No please." He begged, as I pulled the trigger. Then I saw a pile of cash on the table next to the chair, Stewart's fresh corpse occupied. There was easily ten grand I looked around the searching the flat for any other items I could use, that had become surplus to Stewart's requirements. I located a holdall and a further five grand in one of the bedrooms.

As I moved through the hallway, I noticed beer cans strewn across the floor all the way to the kitchen. I spotted the Bunsen burner on the kitchen table. I headed back into the living room. I placed all the money into the holdall, then turned on the gas to Bunsen burner, and the oven before heading out on to the balcony. Closing the door behind me I lit a smoke.

I drew my last drag and flicked the burning dog end through the letter box. I was halfway down the stairs when the gas ignited. The explosion shook the entire block, like a small earthquake. Maybe I didn't need to do that. Ultimately the police would realise it had been murder and that Stewart was dead before the explosion, but then the fire would rid the place of any trace of my being there.

Chapter 24

The hours dragged by. Hampstead Heath was awash with police officers, scene of crime tape, and a large white tent enveloped the spot of P.C Fitzgerald's last breath. Flashing blue lights lit up the tree line, but now faded as the sun rose, washing the area with a natural light. Police officers went about their business, clad in white hooded coveralls, and blue boot covers with matching gloves.

Michael's initial fears had, with the arrival fresh officers, been validated. Hollinson was dead, in the back of Fuller's Jag. A further search of the car had revealed Hollinson's 8 year old Daughter's body in the boot. Fuller despite his protests was immediately arrested on suspicion of murder, along with Daniels who was arrested on a charge of being his accessory. Michael didn't like it, he wanted a result as much as anyone. Fitzgerald was one of their own, but he just couldn't see Fuller and Daniels as cold blooded killers, let alone child killers.

Now Michael and Kate's commanding officer had arrived on scene. Michael knew they were well and truly in the proverbial. DCI Des Langford was a big man with an even bigger presence. In his mid-fifties, with balding grey cropped hair. As he heaved his massive frame from his car, even metres away Michael could see the red glow emanating from Langford's face. As he approached Michael and Kate he unleashed with both barrels.

"WHAT THE ACTUAL FUCK, HAVE YOU PAIR DONE!" He screamed, more at Michael than Kate. Michael had been a copper long enough to know, you fuck up take the bollocking, learn from it and move on. He also knew a fuck up of this magnitude, could spell the end of his career. The higher ups would want a sacrificial lamb as it were. He'd try and protect Kate as the OIC of the pair, he would shoulder as much of the fallout as he could.

Thankfully as the two MI5 agents were now in custody, it would prove harder for them to play the plausible deniability card. Which meant with all said and done, Michael and Kate, with explanations and reprimands issued, were informed rather unceremoniously that an investigation into their conduct would be forthcoming. However, for now they were simply to be reallocated to another case.

"Well, that could have been a lot worse." Stated Kate coldly, as she walked back to the car with Michael. He looked at her with concern etched on his face.

"Kate, a fellow officer is dead, not to mention a child and a judge. How much worse could it have gone?" Michael looked for any sign of emotion. He found none. It's no secret the best coppers can cut off from their emotions, so not to be emotionally involved with cases, victims, or even offenders, but this wasn't, couldn't be a healthy response to what they had both witnessed.

"And they're someone else's problem now." Kate informed him.

"Now let's get back to the station and grab a new case."
With that Kate jumped in the car. Maybe it was shock,
Michael thought as he joined her.

Chapter 25

As I pulled away from Stewart's burning flat, I could
already hear the sound of incoming sirens. I drove for 10
maybe 15 minutes, just putting some distance between me
and, the now probably smouldering, murder scene. I
ditched the car. I thought about paying Paulie a visit, but
without the car, it would take me over an hour to walk.
Also, I was finding it hard to get Carly out of my head. As I
was about a fifteen minute walk from the pub, my choice
was clear. Once I got there, I'd call Liz, using my phone in
the area would help bolster Ray's offer of an alibi.

I was back at the pub in about ten minutes, after running
some of the way, again I was definitely not as fit as I once
was. I sat outside the pub for five minutes, whilst I caught
my breath, and allowed the majority of the last few days,

violent events to sink in. I composed myself, lit a cigarette, and called Liz. She informed me she'd dropped Lacey off at nursery, with Ali. I told her I'd be back shortly after lunch, as I had a few more errands to run. Liz told me to be careful.

"I always am." I told her and hung up.

I walked into the pub's bar area, Carly was stood polishing glasses.

"Jim, you came back." She beamed at me excitedly. I knew then I was definitely falling for this woman.

"What can I say, I just had to see that smile of yours." I smiled as she giggled, and I'm sure she even blushed a little. I asked where her dad was.

"He's out the back." She stated directing me to the door behind her, before offering me a drink. I took her up on it, as fuck I needed one, or ten.

I stepped into the backroom. Ray was stood in the kitchen, with his back to me. He was clearly on the phone, it sounded important, then in a second, I was reaching for my gun!

"Yes, he knows! Everything!" Ray stated down the phone, unaware of his captive armed audience. Was he really in on this?

"Because I fucking told him Paul!" I placed my gun, I was definitely going to have to pay Paulie a visit. Then Ray turned around with a shocked look on his face. With a number of excuses, he ended the call. Then he locked eyes with me.

"I need a fucking drink!" He stated and went to walk past me, but I put my hand on his chest to stop him.

"And I think we need a fucking chat!" I told him sternly.

I allowed my anger to simmer, as I lit a smoke and nursed my whisky, as Ray explained himself. It turned out to be more innocent, than it had sounded. That was if I believed a word of Ray was telling me. Which was that he had simply been making sure, Paulie was ready to hand over the family business to me. I told him clearly, I wasn't interested in being a gangster, I just wanted to clear this whole mess up.

"I'm only working for Paul, because I owe him. I have a business, and its doing alright, and it's legal." I informed him. Ray tried his best to convince me to rethink. I simply told him about Michael's chosen profession, and of my aversion to drugs and junkies alike.

"Leave the drugs to Paul. To be fair your old man and I were never involved in that shit." He was still trying, but for all my criminal activities I wasn't some Sicilian Don.

There were more pressing issues anyway.

"Ray, what do you know about John O'Grady?" My current, and other than Paul, my only lead.

"Not a lot, he came up after your dad died. I heard he was very well connected." He responded. I pressed on.

"Connected? To who? I've only ever heard of him as a club owner." Ray looked at me incredulously.

"He's fucking Irish mob. I'm sorry Jim, but I didn't realise you were so naive." My anger rose up again. I was a few things naïve was not one of them.

"Excuse me Ray, but I'm an ex-soldier, not fucking Sherlock Holmes. I've only been in this seedy little world of yours a short time. My gangster radar ain't perfectly attuned." I told him.

"I'm sorry Jim. I forget you've only been involved with Paulie, and I should know he wouldn't tell you about O'Grady. Even Pauls shit scared of him." That settled it O'Grady needed a meet as well.

Chapter 26

When Michael and Kate got back to the station it was clear the next case wasn't far from their desks. The office was in chaos. Officers were running around in all directions. Phones were ringing off the hook. It looked like something big was going on! Michael hadn't seen this place this busy, not since the 7/7 bombings! Just the thought made Michael's blood run cold. It wasn't long before a young P.C approach Michael with an explanation, and an address. An explosion in a block of flats. A heavily populated block of flats!

"Kate don't get comfortable! We're off!" He declared, grabbing her hand and dragging her from the office.

Upon their arrival, a uniformed Sergeant approached. She was just over 40, with a blonde greying bob.

"D.S Denim, we've got a suspected drugs lab explosion, on the second floor. So far, we have one confirmed fatality." Explained the five foot stout, stern looking Sergeant. That was when a SOCO officer ran over.

"Sarge, your gonna want to hear this! Coroner says our fatality was dead before the explosion!" Declared the coverall clad officer. Michael decided now was the time to make his presence felt.

"How do they know that already?" He asked the young lad, who explained although the body was badly burnt, it was clear the victim had been shot multiple times.

"Any witness'?" Kate dived in.

"One potentially, young girl over there speaking with P.C Davis." Stated the SOCO lad. Michael and Kate walked over to where the girl was giving a statement. Michael gave the P.C a nod inviting her to wrap up her current questioning and join them away from the witness.

P.C Davis was new to the force, she was 24 and fresh out of university, and she had ambitions! Once her probation was done, she would join SOCO then forensics, one day she knew she would be a Super Intendant, bar minimum!

She was tall and slim, and aware many didn't consider her "built for walking the beat." She was an attractive brunette, and admittedly lucky not to have been in any overly dangerous situations, yet.

"P.C Davis, what's our witness saying?" Asked Michael, flashing his I.D.

"She's mentioned a Paul Shawcross being here for a meeting." Michael paused, could she mean the Paulie Shawcross?! Today's trajectory could take a massive shift in direction for Michael and Kate, if they could tie this to him!

"Anything else, have we I. D'd the Vic?" Kate quizzed the young P.C.

"Yes, the victim we believe is a Stewart Dunn. He's the owner of the flat, and the witness' boyfriend." P.C Davis continued.

"According to our witness, he had a meeting with Mr Shawcross this morning, who convinced our witness to leave the property, to go the shop for milk. When she returned, Mr Shawcross was gone, and the flat was on fire." Davis concluded.

"That's great P.C Davis. Do you mind if I take over? Or do you wish to continue your interview?" Michael asked her.

"I'd be more than happy to handover, if I could maybe take notes." Was her response. Michael agreed, and together they approached their witness.

The interview didn't get off to a great start. The witness Rachel saw D.S Denim, and fear spread across her face! It was clear she recognised him and not in a good way. Michael tried to think, had he arrested her before? No, it wasn't that, but something about his presence had this young girl spooked. Then came his answer.

"Mr Shawcross?" Rachel asked. Michael gave Kate a shocked look. Kate simply shrugged in response.

"No miss, my names D.S Mike Denim." Rachel simply starred at him, before saying.

"You look just like him but if he'd had a shave and cut his hair." That settled it. She wasn't describing Shawcross, she was describing his brother Jimmy! What the fuck had Jimmy done now? From the look on Kate's face, she'd drawn the same conclusion. They were fucked! It was a definite conflict of interest!

"If you could give us a moment Miss?" Kate asked, taking hold of Michael's arm and leading him out of earshot.

"I'm not giving up another case today boss!" She stated quite forcefully.

"I don't expect you too. I don't suppose this girl's word would be enough to warrant a positive I.D anyway." Michael responded. He was clutching at straws, and he knew it.

"It does place your brother a two murder scenes, in the space of three days though Mike." Kate looked full of concern, as she spoke. Michael acknowledged this fact, and they agreed to have a meeting with Jimmy, with the first sign of his involvement leading to Michael taking himself of the case.

Chapter 27

I lit a cigarette and poured myself another whisky. I was trying to build up to paying Paulie a visit. I knew I was going to need serious backup, and that meant finally coming clean with Michael and Ali. Obviously, Ali would be easier to get on board than Michael, and he wouldn't be happy, but we'd served together. We'd been through much worse than this. Telling Michael that was a completely different kettle of fish. D.S Michael Denim, how do I tell my Detective Sergeant Brother, that I'm a killer? I would be asking Mike to make a hell of a choice, and if I was completely honest with myself, I really wasn't sure telling my brother the truth wouldn't end with my incarceration!

Ultimately, I knew, I couldn't take on two different gangsters on my own. So, I lit another smoke, and poured another drink. I took out my phone and called Ali. I didn't want to drag him into this, that's why I'd kept quiet about Paulie in the first place, but needs must. After a brief chat we agreed to meet at the office in a few hours. I wasn't going to make my confession on the phone. It was something that needed to be done in person.

I stubbed out my smoke in one of Ray's glass ashtrays. Still trying to work out my next move. As Carly poked her head around the doorway.

"How are you bearing up Jim?" I looked up in response to her question.

"I'll be fine, just compartmentalising. I'm quite good at it." I laughed.

"Shouldn't it be me checking on you?" I asked genuinely concerned after her trauma 12 hours previous, especially knowing she wouldn't have had to endure that experience if it wasn't for my presence.

"I'm good thanks Jim, you're not the one who can compart... what you said." We both laughed, she was an impressively strong woman, and it just made me love her more. We sat and chatted for a while. I wasn't sure if it was the recently shared violence/trauma, with me turning into her saviour twice in a matter of hours, or if it was something else but I felt I'd known her forever. Somehow, I thought Ray wouldn't approve, but I no longer cared. I was already intoxicated by Carly, and her constant longing stares. I wanted to kiss her, then Ray walked in.

"If you pair can pull yourselves away from each other for five minutes I've got to run to the cash and carry." He announced.

"Carly if you can have this place open, for 11 it'd be appreciated." He said turning to me.

"I won't be here when you get back Ray. I'm meeting with my business partner, about 11. So, thanks for all your help." I stated.

"You're alright Jim. I hope you get this mess sorted and stay safe." He told me shaking my hand.

Once Ray had left, Carly offered me a cup of coffee. Well, "offered" was a strong word, I got the distinct impression I didn't have much of a choice in the matter.

"If you ask me, it should be us thanking you for everything you've done." Carly informed me as she passed the hot sobering beverage.

"If it weren't for you, I could've been dead twice over." She added, as she brushed a loose tussle of hair from her face. Then she kissed me.

The kiss was electric. As we embraced, I'd never wanted anyone so much. I wish the moment could last forever and knowing that it couldn't hurt immensely. I pulled away.

"I'm sorry, I shouldn't have done that." Carly apologised.

"Don't be I've wanted to since I met you." I admitted, realising instantly how sappy I now sounded.

"I want you to come back, I know where you've got to go, what you have to do. It could kill you. I just thought, if I didn't kiss you know, I may not get another chance later." She confessed. I fixed her with as strong a gaze as I could manage.

"I'm coming back." I promised, although I knew I couldn't be sure. Carly was right. No matter how you put it, the next few hours could, and more than likely would, see me dead or imprisoned for a severely long time.

I pulled her close again and kissed her tenderly.

"I'm coming back, it's going to take a lot more than a couple of ageing back alley gangsters to take me down." I assured her. The police on the other hand, they definitely had the resources to fuck my entire life.

"I know. You're going now, aren't you?" She asked. I told her I was, then before I knew it, I told her I loved her. "SHIT! Too soon you absolute bell end!" I thought, until she said it back. I kissed her again grabbed the holdall and left. Leaving Carly was almost impossible, and it hurt more than I ever thought it could. It was also going to make everything I had to do a lot harder. I was going to struggle to get Carly out of my head.

I walked back to the car I abandoned earlier. It took fifteen minutes, as I didn't run any of the route this time. There was no clear police presence around the car, so I jumped in and drove back to the office. My phone rang briefly once on my journey, I didn't answer, as I was driving. Not to mention several times over the limit! When I parked, I checked the phone? It was Liz. I hit the re-dial but was sent straight to voicemail. She could've been on the phone to someone else, or her battery may have died, but my gut told me to get home. I jumped back in the car, calling Ali as I did so. It was a brief call, I told him I'd be back in an hour, and sped off home.

As I arrived at Liz's home, I knew something was wrong. The front door was wide open. As I jumped out my car, a wave of nausea coursed over my body. I sprinted to the house calling out to Liz, but I knew it was pointless. As soon as I reached the hallway. Parallel with the stairs, I could see a bloody hand print on the wall. I yanked the Gloch from my waistband, and bolted up the stairs, traversing them two at a time.

I found Liz's phone laying on the floor just outside the master bedroom. A nervous bile billed up my throat. I swallowed hard. The house was silent, and the closer I got to the bedroom the smell of blood and death, grew stronger. I stopped at the doorway. Struggling to keep my legs under me!

I couldn't bear to look inside. I knew what I was going to find or so I thought, and that thought had me completely frozen. I swallowed hard, closed my eyes and took a deep breath. Then I turned into room.

My stomach lurched again, vomit filled my mouth. Liz laid there on the bed. The room itself was immaculate. There was absolutely no sign of struggle, but Liz was dead. Murdered, violently, and I instantly knew by whom!

There she was her naked body almost grey in colour. She was covered in small cuts, and a crucifix carved in to her neck. I fell to my knees. I thought of what Michael had told me about the Priest, just two days ago. The more I thought of it the more I knew my conclusion was bang on the money. The worst part was, I couldn't stop thinking how much worse this could've been. I mean obviously I was devastated by what I was seeing, I still cared about Liz, she had been my wife. However, I couldn't help feeling relieved Lacey wasn't here. It meant she was at nursery and safe! But the thought kept coming back, what if she hadn't been?!

Eventually I managed to drag myself to my feet. I grabbed at my phone, but my hands wouldn't cooperate. They were shaking so violently. I clambered unsteadily down the stairs. Making my way to the kitchen. I went straight to the traditional booze cupboard, every parent has one. I spied a bottle of vodka. I hate the stuff, but guessed it'd do in a pinch! I removed the lid and gulped down hard from the bottle. I lit a smoke, my hands still trembling. I called Michael. He answered on the first ring.

"Where the FUCK are you? And WHAT THE FUCK HAVE YOU BEEN UP TOO?" He screamed.

"I'm at the house, Christ it's bad Mike. I need help." I told him. I was really struggling to hold it together, as Michael fell into a stunned silence.

"It's Liz, Mike. She's dead!" My voice cracked, I was starting to panic.

"We're on our way, and Jimmy, don't move and don't touch a god damn thing!" his commands came barked in cold accusatory tones, and he hung up. The devastation kept coming, now my Brother suspected me of killing my ex-wife!

*   *   *

Michael looked at Kate, she could see the anger radiating off him.

"We've gotta go Kate!" He stated bluntly. He jumped into the unmarked police Astra. His knuckles turning white, as he gripped the steering wheel. Kate ran round to the passenger side and joined him.

"What's going on boss?" She enquired, she was growing more concerned for her partner. Every turn they'd made these last few days, had landed them in more trouble. Now with his Brother somehow involved in all this, she was beginning to wonder what the stress would do to him.

"My Sister-in-law's dead." He replied, as he slammed the car into gear and sped away!

*   *   *

I thought about doing as Michael had told me to, but fear of incarceration urged me to defy him. Either way I felt more and more sure, the deeper I got into the murder of our parents, the closer I came to confronting my last stand. One way or another, there were few options left, and they were dwindling by the minute. If I was honest my life, as I knew it was over. Either Shawcross or O'Grady was in league with the Priest, and I now suspected that was who had attacked Carly, and now one or both of them were coming after me. As was my Brother, and with him the long arm of the law.

I didn't have long, but I had to put a plan into action. If I simply ran, I'd be caught in no time at all. I contacted Carly to ask if she could collect and take care of Lacey. She agreed, so my next point of call, was Lacey's nursery. They weren't happy but I didn't give them much choice. Then I had to speak to Ali. I left the house as I'd found it. When Michael arrived, he'd bring in a swarm of plods, and I didn't want to contaminate any evidence.

Chapter28

Ray hated lying to Carly, but it seemed better if she didn't know he was going to put himself at this much risk, for a man they barely knew, but it seemed his only option.

If he could hash this out, with Paulie, maybe he could save Jimmy a job. So here he was, pulling up outside Paulie's mansion, he felt an anger rise in him, as he thought Barry, would never be so flashy! Ray removed his tie, and rolled up his sleeves, before exiting the car. He stood unmoving for a moment simply content to eyeball Harry.

"You want something Ray? Or you happy admiring the view?" It was Harry who broke the silence.

"I'm sorry Harry, I thought I'd stumbled upon a specialist zoo!" Ray responded with chuckle.

"You cheeky old cunt." Was Harry's witty retort.

"I've come to see Paulie, you ugly old bastard." Ray stated no longer smiling. Neither was Harry.

"You armed Ray?" Harry questioned. Ray assured him he wasn't and after a rough, but quick frisk, Harry invited Ray in.

They walked the hallway, reminiscing about the good old days. As Ray quizzed Harry about the young scantily clad girls, adorning the walls.

"Business is good, remember we could've got through a few in our younger days, eh Ray?" Laughed Harry. Ray just flashed a fake smile, he'd never liked the idea of the old gang involving themselves with basses.

As they approached Paul's office, Harry stopped indicating to Ray to follow suit.

"Why'd you do it Ray? Why'd you have to open your mouth, to the boy?" Harry asked, clearly not actually wanting an answer as he continued, with only a slight pause.

"I like Jim, he was a good lad. Me and Frank don't want to have to hurt either of you." He stated, opening the door.

As they stepped through the entrance, Ray knew he'd fucked up. Paul was sat at his large mahogany desk, a look of Al Pacino in Scarface about him. He was smoking a Cuban and drinking a Scotch.

"Ray my old mucker, how've you been?" He asked with a wicked smile. That was when Ray saw Frank, as he turned in what would prove to be a futile attempt to defend himself, Harry's right arm wrapped around his throat, he was done. Harry held Ray in a choke. The room grew dark, and Ray cursed at his own stupidity, as he lost consciousness.

Chapter 29

As Michael and Kate pulled up outside, Jimmy and Liz's old home, Michael tried Jimmy's phone. There was no answer.

"Fuck it! He's running!" He stated with exasperation. Kate looked at him, he was losing it. With all Jimmy's actions, Kate was becoming more convinced of his guilt, but Kate felt for him.

"We still need to go in and check it out." She advised. Michael sighed heavily and nodded in agreement. They exited the vehicle, as they did, they adorned latex gloves. The pair made their way through the open door. The smell of blood and death now enveloped the house.

"Check the living room, and the other rooms down here." Instructed the D.S.

"I'll check upstairs." He offered, making his way to the upper floor.

As he reached the top of the stairs, the stench of death was definitely stronger. Nausea took hold. Then he saw her. He called to Kate, whilst using the doorframe to steady himself. All the colour drained from his face. Dread snuck up on him. What if his Niece was here? This was definitely the work of the Priest, and history showed with every adult, this piece of shit murdered, there would be a child not far away! Michael knew that would end everything. If this bastard had touched Lacey! If he had to see his beautiful Niece like this, if he had to find her. He'd string this bastard up by his bollocks himself. Then it hit him, if he would react like this, then maybe that's how Jimmy had gotten involved. If that were the case, Michael could never bring him in.

Michael turned away from the room as Kate reached the top step.

"It wasn't Jim. It was him again!" He informed her.

"I hate to admit it, but we could do with Fuller and Daniels." He added.

"We've got to call this in now Guv. This Priest thing is getting out of hand, this is six bodies now in 3 days!" Kate exclaimed.

"Yeah, you're right, I'll do that, do me a favour Kate check the other rooms up here. If Lacey's here…" He trailed off. Kate nodded in response. She totally understood. She'd secretly loved Michael for years. The Denim's were like family to her. Then she wondered what would she do, if she did find Lacey up here?

Michael made his way downstairs, he pulled out his mobile and called the DCI.

"Boss, I need you to release the B.O.S Agents." Michael explained, through DCI Langford's rants about Michael and Kate being off the case.

"We know that boss, it's just the Priest's latest victim is my Sister-in-law!" He declared.

"Jesus Christ! O.K Denim, wait there secure the scene I'm on my way, and I'll bring the Agents." He finally conceded.

Kate ran down the stairs Michael felt his stomach lurch up into his chest.

"It's clear boss Lacey's not here. Thank Christ!" She said running into Michael's embrace.

A simple "Thank Fuck" was all Michael could manage in response.

Chapter 30

I reached the office not long before midday. The sun was hot, I thought of Liz. The indignity of death would, unfortunately be in full swing by now. I could imagine the smell would be horrific in this heat. I walked into the office, I needed to talk with Ali, and the sooner the better. I was beginning to feel exhausted, but I had to power through.

Ali was sat at his desk, he looked as tired as I felt.

"Hey bud, I think we need to talk." I told him. I realised looking at him then I'd been a selfish prick, and a shitty friend, these last few days. In fact, I could probably say most of my life, but the last few days I'd really put Ali out.

"Yeah, no worries, mate, how's everything panning out, got any leads on the Wyman thing?" Ali really was the best bloke out there; I'd been an absolute cunt! From the moment we'd met he'd always had my back.

"A few, but it's me we need to talk about mate." I don't know how I had the nerve to call him mate.

"I fucked up man, more than normal, I've killed people." I confessed.

"I know mate I was there for some of them." He laughed.

"Ali, I mean since, we started the business. We were close to folding, and I got us a bail out from an old associate from before the army. The money kept us going, but it had a price." I explained.

"That's Shawcross, right?" He asked, more as a suggestion than a question. I just stared at him, possibly open mouthed.

"I'm a P.I Jim, and he approached me too." He confessed.

We talked for an hour; I couldn't believe Ali had known what I'd been doing this whole time. I updated him on everything from the last few days. I finished by telling him about Liz.

"Shit, I'm sorry mate, what do you need?" He asked. The moment of truth.

"I think I know who ordered it. I know the Priest killed her, and I think Paulie ordered it." I told him.

"I can't get to him on my own. Believe me mate I wouldn't ask if I wasn't desperate." I implored him.

"I know mate, I know because you've worked so hard to keep me out of your dealings with Paulie, until now." Ali paused with his response. I knew what came next.

"You know if we do this, that's it! Neither of us can stay here." It hurt, but I knew he was right.

It was the one outcome I hadn't given much thought. If I somehow survived all this, and avoided capture by the police, which I did think was the odds-on favourite. Leaving the country was a possibility.

"I hear Miami's nice, all year round." Ali chuckled. I looked at him.

"Really? I always had you down as a Bahamas type of guy." I joked. With that the conversation returned to a serious nature. This op would need serious planning. The last thing I wanted was to get Ali hurt, even though I had to admit, up until now I hadn't given the repercussions to Ali much, if any, consideration. I really was a shitty friend!

"So how are arming ourselves?" Ali asked, I explained that Paulie owned a lock up on the estate. I'm sure I saw his eyes light up, at the mention of MP5s. His eyes definitely lit up, when I told him about the pump action shotgun.

"All fucking right then! Let's get these bastards!" Ali was clearly chomping at the bit. It was the first time I realised Ali had missed the action as much as I did.

Seeing how much Ali missed soldiering, hurt a lot more than I'd thought it would. After his injury I had been sure he was happy with his decision to leave the life. Now it was clear he'd missed it, or was it just bravado? The thing was I'd never know.

Chapter 31

Paulie paced up and down his office, occasionally glaring at Ray's unconscious body. With barely veiled contempt. He still couldn't believe Ray had grassed him up. After all these years, the whole Denim debacle had laid dormant. Now a "friend" of some 40 years had thrown him under the bus at the first opportunity, and now Paulie was in the shit, with men he'd worked so hard to keep onside. Now he'd been ordered to clean up the loose ends. Ray would be easy, the bastard was a snitch, and had to go, but Jimmy was another matter altogether.

Paul respected Jimmy maybe even feared him a little. Jimmy was a unique individual, a cold-blooded killer whom you could rely on. He was loyal, but if he decided there would be little Paul could do to stay alive. Paulie and his crew were emotionally invested in Jimmy. He was likeable but word had come down. He had to go, but how?

Then Ray began to stir, Harry and Frank had adorned Ray's immediate surroundings in tarpaulin, and Ray had been tied to a chair. Paul pounced immediately, punching Ray hard in the face, before roughly grabbing his hair and leaning in close.

"What did you tell him?" Paul asked out right. Ray spat a mouthful of blood onto the tarp, his head already spinning.

"You already know what I told him!" Ray stated defiantly, feeling his mouth refill with blood.

"Why'd you have to do it Ray? We've looked after you. You stupid cunt!" Paul let the venom drip on every word.

"Because you slags tried to rape and murder my daughter! And if that ain't good enough, Barry was my friend. He didn't deserve what those bastards did to him!" Ray informed him through claret filled spittle. Ray knew what was coming, it was over, but he'd die knowing Jimmy would dispatch every mug involved, Paulie included, but that didn't help with the fucking shaking!

Paulie lifted Ray's head.

"I'm sorry it had to come to this Ray, but you have my word, no one touches Carly. The mistake lies with you, and it dies with you." Paulie stated as he pulled a knife from his waistband. Ray simply stared at him defiantly! Paulie leaned in and apologised again, as he slipped the blade into Ray's chest, and watched as the life drained out of Ray's eyes. Then he called in Harry and Frank. They would dispose of Ray's lifeless corpse.

Chapter 32

The car had adopted an ominous silence as Ali pulled up towards Paulie's mansion. Something didn't sit right as the car came to a halt. The house looked quiet, and Harry wasn't stood at the front door. Something was going on. Ali fixed me with a glance as he pulled on a balaclava, on my orders no need for him to get I. D'd.

We jumped out the car, Ali retrieved an enforcer from the back seat, as I lifted the boot revealing the small armoury, we'd liberated from Paulie's own personal lock up. We divvied up the weaponry, 2 flash bangs, 2 MP5s, 2 Glochs, Tac knives, and loaded magazines, then made our way to the door. I flicked the pin from my first flash bang, and shoved it through the letterbox, just as Ali slammed the enforcer into the lock. I heard the flash bang discharge followed by a thud. Ali attacked the lock again with the enforcer, this time it gave, a testament to Ali's sheer power. We raised the MP5s and made our way through the foyer.

Harry and Frank stumbled around dazed and confused. Something wrapped in tarpaulin lay on the floor between them. I gently squeezed the trigger of my MP5 putting 3 rounds into Frank's chest. His body bucked with each bullet as they hit! Harry's confusion quickly switched to panic reaching for a pistol, in his concealed shoulder holster, but Ali was far too quick, 2 shots rang out from Ali's MP5.

Harry's legs seemed to buckle on him as he hit the ground, and Ali dived on him, pulling his gun arm free and slamming a knee into his ribs. It took me a second to realize that Ali had aimed for his legs. Ali had made sure to disarm Harry quickly, before wrenching him up and slamming him into the closest wall.

"How many more of you cunts are there?" Ali quizzed the ageing gangster. I wondered if Ali still had the killer instinct, and if he didn't, had I made the right choice involving him? I replaced the safety on my MP5 and removed the Gloch from my waistband.

"Maybe you'll find out before you die you fucking mug!" Came Harry's defiant response, Ali struck again with his knee, this time targeting Harry's groin.

I approached the tarpaulin, uncovering whatever it was desperately trying to conceal. The sight of Ray's face hit me like a sledgehammer, I hadn't fully intended to kill Paulie, I had hoped he would've helped, but by killing Ray he'd confirmed my worst fear. The men I'd been working for had definitely had a hand in my parent's murders.

"We can, and we will kill you and any other slag we come across, now how many?" Ali demanded the answer raising his MP5 barrel to meet Harry's chin. I didn't give him a chance, I walked over lifting my Gloch, a single shot struck Harry in the temple his face frozen in shock as Ali released his grip, on the lifeless sack of shit. Ray and Carly's faces filled my head. What the fuck had I done?

"What the fuck was that, Jim?" Ali asked incredulously.

"They killed Ray." I stated solemnly pointing to the tarp wrapped corpse. Ali knew instinctively I would blame myself, but we both knew we couldn't switch off, if we did, we would both join Ray in the tarp!

After that incredibly short explanation, we pushed on. I knew Paulie would be in his office, but he'd be prepared for me, so Ali suggested he approach the office from the outside, I agreed and gave Ali a quick set of directions.

*　　　　　*　　　　　*

Ali headed outside Paulie's mansion, pausing to pick up his earlier discarded enforcer. Cautiously he made his way around to Paulie's office, making sure to check the corners. He couldn't help but think this was all going too easy, nor was he overly happy with how easy Jimmy had dispatched two men, he'd previously called friends. It was concerning at best! Ali pushed on, then he saw it, ducking behind a large rose bush.

Paulie's office looked out over his pristinely kept gardens, from a pair of bay windows. Ali could see Paulie scrambling around his office. Clearly arming himself, preparing for the inevitable attack. Ali took a moment to calm himself, it had been years since he'd been involved in a fire fight! He prepped his flash bang, pulled the pin and launched it through the bay windows. Instantly Ali reached for another flash bang, the first exploded, he threw the second as another blinding explosion filled Paulie's office!

Following the third phosphorus explosion Ali climbed up slamming the enforcer into the window panel.

*　　　　　*　　　　　*

Paulie heard the explosion ring out. It sounded like it had come from the front door. The initial explosion was followed by the tell-tale sound of gun shots. Paulie hadn't heard any shouts of "Armed Police", but maybe he was mistaken. After all he knew Harry and Frank would've been in the foyer, with Ray's corpse!

Paul opened his office wall safe, there was a quarter of a million in £50 notes, the stacks of cash surrounded what Paul was really searching for. Paul grabbed at the silver Desert Eagle with black handle. Just as he inserted the magazine and charged the weapon, all hell broke loose!

The window behind Paul smashed. He jumped behind the table, but his office door opened, just a fraction, and a gloved hand rolled a black cylinder into the room, SHIT! He was fucked. Paulie just narrowly avoided being blinded by the first tac grenade, but they had him surrounded, and the second he took full on, as he did the third! Paul's eyes burned and his ears rang, before he knew what was happening, he was being manhandled across the room!

   *   *   *

As Ali left, I headed through the house, my MP5 lifted in a firing position. Maybe I hadn't needed Ali in on this, I thought as I met no resistance on my route to Paulie's office.

I crouched by the door to Paul's office, placing a hand on the door handle and listening for Ali's arrival. I heard the sound of shattering glass. I pulled my tac grenade from my belt, pulling the pin with teeth, like I'd seen numerous actors do in war and action films over the years. I eased the door open and rolled the explosive cannister into the middle of his office and took cover!

As I heard the third, I knew it was game time! I flung the door open and saw Paulie on the deck. He was on all fours patting the floor, clearly blind and unaware of my presence. I could have easily killed him there and then, but then I saw what he was searching for, just before he got within a metre of it. I kicked the Desert Eagle across the room and grabbed the back of his collar. In what felt like one fluid movement, I lifted him up off of the floor, and shoved him hard into the wall, resting my forearm on his throat!

Then the window flung open, and Ali climbed through. He simply strode over and planted a big right hand on Paulie's chin. Paulie dropped as the force of the blow caused me to lose my grip on him. Ali cable tied Paul's wrists and ankles together, whilst I spotted the safe still open. Fuck me I'd never seen so much cash in one place. We grabbed a holdall and emptied the contents of the safe into it. Ali swung Paulie over his shoulder, and we made our way back out to the car.

We clocked the sound of sirens as Ali shoved Paulie heavily into the back of the car. We dumped the guns in the boot and sped off. Putting plenty of distance between us, the mansion and the old bill!

Chapter 33

The investigation into Liz's untimely death was reaching the end of it's second hour. D.S Denim and D.C Marshall were still on scene. With Michael eager to get out. The house was full of SOCO coppers. Michael really wanted to find Jimmy and bounce him off several walls! What the fuck was he up to? And what the hell was he dragging Michael into?

It was at that moment the BOS 90 agents arrived. Fuller fixed Michael with an accusatory glare, as Daniels breezed in, instantly talking to members of the SOCO team. Who the fuck did this Fuller prick think he was? Thought Michael, who decided to get his in first.

"They followed my advice then?" Michael opted to ask, alluding to the fact Fuller and Daniels had him to thank for their freedom. He didn't get a response, Fuller brushed past him following Agent Daniels.

This was taking forever, eventually after taking a tour of the entire downstairs of the property, Agent Daniels approached Michael holding a photograph. It was a picture of Jimmy in his para trooper uniform with Lacey.

"D.S Denim?" She asked, "Do you know this man?" Daniels fixed him with a curious look.

"Yeah, he's, my brother. Why?" He was really beginning to dislike these two.

"I know him too, he was in my brothers unit." She stated a slight look of sentiment creeping into her face.

"I don't think you should be here Michael, your too close to this now. Go home I'll explain to your C.O and I promise you we will get this bastard!" She told him sympathetically.

"Thanks, I think you might be right." Michael agreed, but he had no intention of going home, or leaving this case alone. No, after this if anyone was going to catch this "Priest" fucker, it was him!

Chapter 34

Once we were sure we hadn't picked up a police tail, me and Ali drove Paulie to his own lock up. I shoved Paulie into place on a chair in the middle of the unit.

"Ali do me a favour, get down to the Occasional Half, it's on Hawthorne Grove. I need you to keep an eye on the barmaid." I half asked half told him. I didn't want him here to see what I was about to do to my former employer.

"The barmaid?" Ali asked incredulously. "Yeah, her names Carly, her dad's the boke this cunt had in the tarp!" I explained "Right enough said." It was although I could see the worry in his face. Along with the disappointment.

Paulie started to stir as Ali drove off, I pulled the door shut and collected a blow torch from the shelf. I strode confidently towards Paul lighting the blow torch upon my approach.

"So, Mr Shawcross I've got a few questions for you." I informed him as I lowered the blow torch towards his fear field face.

"Why did you kill Ray?" I asked my voice deadly calm. Shawcross looked at me with disdain.

"I done him because he was a grass now get that fucking thing out my face!" He declared trying to wrestle some control back. I drew the blow torch closer, so the flame brushed his cheek. The skin bubbled underneath the heat. He tried briefly to contain the pain, but it was never going to happen I remove the heat as he let out a deafening scream.

"Who are you working for? And what does my family have to do with any of this?" I pushed on you now from Ray, Paulie work directly for whoever was behind all of this.

"And what end up like Ray! You can go fuck yourself!" He declared defiantly. I smiled, too fucking late for that! I thought almost out loud. I simply brushed the flame of the torch over his right hand. He didn't resist the pain this time. The unit filled with the smell of burnt bacon, and Paul's blood curling screams.

"Tell me what I want to know maybe I get to these cunts before you they get you!" I stared straight him straight in the eyes.

"If you don't tell me, I guarantee you it will wind up like Ray!" I informed him coldly. The bastard laughed, clearly racked with pain but still he laughed.

"You kill me and then you want O'Grady and your father-in-law, but you won't last!" He chuckled

"You're a fucking dead man Jim. Shame I really liked you, but your fucking dead." He laughed hard my anger simmered. I pulled my Gloch from my waistband and pointed it at his face. Defiantly he leaned forward engulfing the barrel in his mouth, his eyes locked on mine. I pulled the trigger and watched as his eyes dulled, and the back of his head exploded.

Chapter 35

It didn't take Ali long to find the occasional half he pulled up just as Carly, at least Ali believed it was Carly, returned to the pub with Lacey in tow.

"Carly?" Ali called out, almost asking. She looked up she looked terrified by the hulking giant approaching her, on the young child she had only just met upon collecting her from nursery, until the child spoke.

"Uncle Ali!" Came the child's shrill call. Lacey ran past Carly and into Ali's massive waiting arms.

"Hello pickle." Ali responded he loved his God daughter more than anyone in the world, considering her cheery tone he knew she didn't know about her mum yet. He didn't envy the person who had to have that conversation. With that being said someone also had to inform Carly about ray. Ali hoped Jimmy wouldn't be too much longer.

As Carly unlocked the doors to the pub, She asked Ali if he could help with the bar. Ali agreed, eat always quite fancies running a pub. So, they set Lacey up near the bar with pens, paper, and a bottle of coke as regulars started meandering in.

Chapter 36

Kruger laid on the Lilo, floating in his pool. He had one of these men, poor him a whiskey. The last few days had been incredibly stressful. Even the young girl Gregor had arranged for him the previous night, hadn't left him completely satisfied. There was only one thing that could bring that feeling of elation now, and that was the confirmation of that bastard Denim boy's overdue demise. A job which was becoming apparent, that was too much for the priest.

Kruger knew now he had to bring in another of his and Gregor's favoured professionals. He was sure the Irishman would make short work of the fucking up start. Gregor had been on his case since Wyman had started all this mess. Marcus hated fucking snitches. He was happy to hear about Ray Valentine, hopefully Shawcross would lead denim straight to the Irishman, and if he was able to kill him, he'd pay him double.

Chapter 37

me our it took me to walk back to the pub, I made the decision's that needed to be made. We split the 250,000 pounds between me, Ali, and Carly, I'd take 50,000 pounds just to set myself up in America. This made sense as I'd dragged Carla and Ali into this mess, I had to make sure they were set. I'd also decided on California for my retirement.

As I walked into the pub I was confronted by mixed greetings by Lacey, and Carly, clearly couldn't have been happier to see me. Ali, however had a look of concern and disapproval. Lacey ran over and jumped into my arms, Carly did similar whilst I continued to hug Lacy. Ali reminds behind the bar.

"Whiskey?" Ali asked me I definitely needed it, I looked at Carly as I answered.

"And a shower, if that's OK Carly." She informed me it was fine. I guessed it was probably clear to everyone that I needed it.

Carla took me upstairs, as soon as Ali had passed me the whiskey. On the way up she passed me towels, and said she'd grab me some of her dad's clothes. Christ I still had to have those conversations yet. I drank the whiskey and jumped in the shower. After drying off I headed into Ray's room, wake Carly had laid out a pair of jeans, and a black shirt. I pulled on the jeans and sat on the edge of the bed. It didn't take long before I fell back on the bed, and everything faded to black.

I was woken by Carly, she looked worried, and explained she was about to make something for Lacey to eat and wanted to know if there was anything she couldn't have. I said there wasn't, but we did need a chat. I had to tell her about ray, I'd meant to do it straight after my shower. I thought that must have been what she was worrying about.

As Carly made Lacey dinner, I grabbed a bottle of whiskey and two glasses, I had a feeling we were going to need it Ali was more than happy tending bar. Carly broached the subject of Ray's absence stating he'd left for the cash and carry that morning, and she worried something had happened, my gut lurched.

Carly that's what we need to talk about. I said solemnly. I explained how I found ray at Paulie's mansion, and how I'd killed Paulie, frank and Harry. She broke down crying into my chest. I apologised for not making it in time, if I'd known he was going I'd have warned him off and he'd still be here. Fuck all this and I still had to go through all of this with Lacey!

After a few hours last orders, a tearful bedtime for Lacey, and locking the pub doors, Ali and Carly explained how they explained to Lacey, that she would be living with me now, but hadn't spoke about why. They both advised to leave it a week or so. I agreed. We finished off the bottle of Jack and started talking about the money. I told Carly and Ali to take 100,000 pounds each, and that the 50,000 pounds would be enough to set me up in California.

I told Allie I wanted him to stay put for now. After what Paulie had done, I didn't want to leave Carly and Lacey on their own, and I definitely didn't want him getting in anymore ship because of me. he agreed said he's goodnight's and headed up to Carly's guest room. Then it was just me and Carla.

We continued drinking for a while, before Carly began getting teary again. I patted the seat next to me.

"Come on darling come here." I invited her, she clearly required a cuddle, and said as much as she sat down. I put my arm around there, as she rested her head on my chest. I slowly run my hand through her hair. Within 15 minutes should fallen asleep. I gave it half an hour, before gently lifting her up and carrying her up to a room and play singer on the bed. I softly kissed her forehead and made for the bedroom door.

"Don't leave, please. I don't want to be alone." Carla stud as I took hold of the door handle.

"I'll just check on Lacey, then I'll be right back." I told her softly. She simply smiled at me, as I turned and headed to Lacey's room.

Lacey was sleeping soundly, so I crept up to the bed kissed her head and brushed a truss of her hair from her face. Then I returned to Carly who looked up at me.

thank you. She said as I climbed into bed beside her. As we cuddled, I felt sleep envelop me.

chapter 38

Michael pulled out of the space, I as Kate ran up alongside, and jumped into the car's passenger seat.

"Not leaving without me, were you Gov?" She huffed.

"Shit, sorry Kate, I didn't think." Michael apologised. He explained he had to try and find Jimmy. Guilty or innocent he had a lot of explaining to do, and those explanations could lead to the next piece of the puzzle.

Michael racked his brain for where Jimmy could be. In all honesty he could be anywhere. Then the police radio came to life. reports of gunfire, a property Michael was able to identify as belonging to Paulie Shawcross. He looked at Kate who shook her head.

"Michael no! We should leave it. You're too close to it!" She tried to reason with him.

"Exactly, and I've no fucking idea how or why!" He declared slamming his foot down on the accelerator.

It confused Michael, he driven at high speed with Kate in the car numerous times, but she continued to try and convince him to stand down. He couldn't no matter what Kate used to reason with him. He was up to his neck in this and needed answers.

As they arrived Michael, could see the anger dripping from Kate's cold stare.

"Come on mate, once more into the breach." He smiled but Kate had clearly had a complete sense of humour failure and stared at him. Fuck it he told himself, there were enough police here he didn't need Kate to back him up.

He walked through the door, wiping his warrant card at anyone who tried to challenge his entry. As soon as he got into the house, he knew they had been too late. That he been too late, too slow. Body's littered the foyer. Including one ready wrapped in tarpaulin.

Michael continued his walk around the property. He kept hearing the same thing from the SO19 armed officers, that it could very well have been them that had done this. Michael had noted several, tell-tale signs this had been a very professional job, and incredibly military like. That's when he knew it had been Jimmy, and he had to nick him, no one else would get close to him.

Michael ran to the car, Kate was still obviously pissed at him. He instantly radioed comms asking for a trace on Jimmy's car and mobile.

"We can't go after your brother Michael!" Kate screamed at him.

"The fuck we can't!" Michael responded, but as they pulled into the main road he realised, Kate wasn't talking from a professional standpoint. If she had been, she wouldn't have a gun pointed at Michael's gut!

"Don't make me shoot you Mike." She pleaded with him.

"It's bad enough they going to kill Jimmy, don't force me to kill you too!" She continued.

"Who's they? And what the fuck do you think you're doing Kate?" Responded Mike, slowly increasing his speed.

"Michael if you just keep quiet and leave this case alone. They'll pay you a shit tonne." Kate tried to convince him.

"And then what Kate? Spend the rest of my career taking bribes, or worse live in a pocket of OCG?" Mike asked as the car hit 70.

"It's not like that. I'm not bent Mike! You would never get a conviction on these people, and even if you did, they'd have you killed!" She stated flatly realizing she was fighting a losing battle.

"You can live financially comfortably, or you can die. That's the choice." Kate said her final gambit.

Michael looked Kate dead in the eye, as the car reached 80MPH. Finger tensed on the trigger, but it was all in vain. Michael wrenched the steering wheel hard to the right and ripped up the handbrake. The car tipped to the right at flipped, as Kate pulled the trigger. Michael felt the bullet burn across the front of his left bicep. The roof of the car slammed into the ground. The windscreen shattered covering them both in glass.

Michael opened his eyes as the car came to a stop. He saw the gun below him on the tarmac. He saw Kate panicking, there was blood matting her hair, and she was struggling with her seat belt. It refused to release, Michael hit the red release button on his own seat belt, unscramble the into the car ceiling. Kate screamed at him to help her.

"Go fuck yourself Kate! You can wait for the services." He stated as he climbed through the whole of the windscreen. He kicked the gun away from the car. That's when he noticed the flames igniting on the underside of the engine, which Now appeared to be the top of the car. He scrambled back inside the car, Kate was still hanging in her seat, struggling with her seat belt.

"Kate stops dicking about the cars going to blow!" Mike screamed at her. He reached up for the belt buckle it wouldn't budge. He looked around for anything he could use to cut through the belt. Michael saw the fear in Kate's face, he couldn't help it he was now starting to panic. He crawled back out through the windscreen, looking for something to cut the belt with

As he scoured the road for a piece of glass big enough for the job. Two men ran over and pulled Michael away from the car as it exploded. The flames engulfed the car and smoke filled the street. Michael knew it was hopeless, Kate would have died instantly, and it was his actions that had caused her death.

Chapter 39

The RTC crew arrived at the scene within the hour. Along with DCI Langford. Michael sat at the back of the first ambulance to attend, having his gunshot wound (if you could call it that) looked at. He knew he'd been incredibly lucky. DCI Langford approached DS Denim, a forlorn look on his face. This would be bad news.

"Unfortunate business all this." Langford began.

"Shame about Kate, always thought she was a gooden." He stated frowning.

"So did I Gov." Michael replied, he meant it as well. He'd been in shock from the moment she'd pulled the gun on him, acting solely on instinct.

"Worse now, the whole affair has to be investigated." The DCI continued giving Michael a sympathetic look.

"Which gives me no choice, but to suspend you DS Denim." Mike's gut clenched.

"But I was shot, sir surely this is open and shut!" Mike interjected.

"Also, I'm one lead away from cracking, what appears to be a massive OCG!" He lied clinging to anything he could.

"Look I'm sorry Mike, but this must be done. You'll be on full pay, but another officer has died in the line of her duty, and that means we have an obligation to investigate that!" Langford stated losing his sympathetic tone.

"Line of her duty?! Her duty was to the force, not the fucking OCG's!" Michael bit back.

"That's quite enough, Detective Sergeant!" Langford was now infuriated.

"I'm not going to repeat myself. Once the medics have done with you, I expect you to fuck off home!" Langford's eyes locked on Mike's. It made Mike feel uneasy, and he felt unable to argue back anymore.

So, Michael accepted his fate, and headed home. He would continue his hunt for Jimmy in the morning. Right now, he needed a serious drink!

Chapter 40

It was getting late, and Kreuger was getting more frustrated with the situation. He hadn't heard from Shawcross at all! In fact, all Denim updates had gone infuriatingly fucking quiet!

Marcus made his way to his private gym/dojo. He decided, rather hoped, an hour's workout would relieve some stress. He didn't have much of a workout, before a young Philippino boy, wearing a white vest and red shorts ran through with a ringing phone. He gave the boy a hard stare before ripping the phone from his hand!

It was his man in the police, or at least one of them. The police officer had some news for Marcus, some very upsetting and irritating news! Firstly, it appeared that Shawcross had been kidnapped. It was safe to assume he was dead, thought Marcus. The second part of the update was what hit him hard. Kate Marshall had always been one of his favourite operatives. Now to hear of her death, it was a shame, and to make matters worse it, appeared she'd met her end at the hands of the other fucking Denim!

Marcus launched the phone across the dojo. The Philippino boy, seemed to know what was coming next. He dropped to his knees and covered his face. As Krueger approached him, he started pleading. Almost begging for his life. It wasn't enough. Marcus lifted the boy into the hair by his black hair. Krueger didn't hear the boy's screams. As he punched, kicked, and stamped on the boy. The screams diminished as the boy's blood escaped across the floor of the dojo.

Krueger didn't pause. Using a towel, he wiped the blood from his face and dropped the towel onto the boy's corpse. As he walked through his mansion, he simmered. Klichkov would not appreciate this turn of events. It did confirm what Kreuger had known for years, the Denim's boys had to go!

Chapter 41

I awoke alone. The white satin linen empty, but for myself. Then Carly entered the room, holding two mugs of tea. A man could get used to this, I thought.

"Ali's downstairs with Lacey, I hope you don't mind I made her breakfast." She informed me offering the tea. I reached over the side of the bed, to my trouser pocket, grabbing for my smokes and lighter. Carly took an ashtray from her bedside table and moved it between us on the bed.

I lit my cigarette and offered the pack across to Carly.

"Thanks." She said appreciatively taking one and lighting it herself. I allowed my eyes to wander, over her barely covered body.

"So, what's next?" she asked with a cheeky smile as she caught my longing look.

"Next I need to pay my ex-father-in-law a visit." I had to make sure he knew what had happened to Liz, and Shawcross had clearly had dealings with him. I figured any information he could offer would flow following the death of his daughter at the hands of these animals.

"And, what about when all this is over?" Carly asked.

"I was thinking America, why you want to join?" I asked flashing her a smile. Carly chuckled then fixed me with a serious look.

"Do you mean it?" She asked her brown eyes full of hope.

"I wouldn't leave without you." I assured her. She rested her head on chest.

I took a gulp of tea, and a drag on my smoke.

"Thank you for everything you've done Jim." She said looking up at me. I fixed her with a confused look.

"You didn't kill dad, those bastards did, and it could've been me. Twice over! I won't let those cunts dictate my life like they did my dad's!" She stated.

"I never thought you would, and don't worry. I'll make sure they never dictate anyone's life, ever again!" I told her, holding her tight. She looked up again, this time reaching up with her right hand, pulling my face close to hers, and kissing me hard and passionately. Carly brushed her hands across my bare chest. I pushed her long blonde hair back behind her ear, and softly traced kisses up the side of her neck.

She ran her hands down my chest, running the tips of her fingers over, what was left of my six-pack. She followed her fingers with her lips, kissing her way along my chest. I unbuttoned her shirt, untying the knot above her mid-drift. I lifted her head back level with mine and kissed her hard again, as her hands reached my morning glory. She gripped it stroking slowly under my boxers. I brushed her open shirt back over her shoulders, running my fingers down her arms, as her shirt fell from her beautiful frame, and I cupped her pert breasts brushing her nipples with my thumbs. I moved my hands behind releasing her bra clasp, watching as her bra dropped down her toned arms. I rolled with her on the bed placing her on her back, and softly worked my kisses down her athletic body.

Kissing her collarbone, I softly cupped her soft breasts, running me tongue to her nipple, giving it a playful flick with my tongue. She pulled her down her skirt and pink silk panties. Still tickling her nipples with my tongue, I slowly ran my hand down past her mid-drift, to her already moist sex, she wriggled beneath my touch. Carly let out an inviting gasp, as I ran a finger over, before sliding in it in. I kissed down her stomach, until my head was between her lusciously long legs, which she instinctively wrapped around my neck.

I went to work, with my tongue and fingers. She bit her bottom lip, before letting out an ecstatic moan. We made love for what seemed like an hour, exploring each other's bodies slowly and sensually. Both realising it could be our first and last time together. In reality we were probably in one another's embrace for 20 minutes at best. It felt like we belonged in this moment. We laid in each other's arms, with me still inside her, for another 10-15 minutes.

I kissed her softly before looking her in those beautiful brown eyes.

"That was amazing." I told her I almost told her I loved her but managed to stop myself. She smiled almost as if she had read my mind.

"I was waiting all night for that." She informed me. I laughed I'd thought the same but hadn't wanted to take advantage of the situation, which I still felt partially at fault for.

After looking at the time, we both acknowledged we had to get downstairs. I suggested Carly continue as normal until the police arrived to inform her of Ray's death, it could raise questions if they knew she had already been informed of his death. After speaking with Ali, we all agreed on a plan going forward. I would visit Liz's dad, whilst Carly looked after Lacey, and Ali tended to the pub.

I kissed Carly and Lacey before I left.

"And where's mine?" Ali joked, I grabbed his hand and he pulled me into a hug.

"You stay safe brother." He told me as he held me in his embrace, I knew then he'd forgiven me, my transgressions.

"You too bruv." I replied knowing he'd do everything in his power to keep both girls safe, without me having to ask.

Chapter 42

Michael woke, his head banging, as if a brass marching band had taken up residence. His mouth as dry as the Gobi Desert. He couldn't remember getting home the previous evening, nor what had followed subsequently. What he did know was he had to find Jimmy, who must've been aware that Michael knew exactly what had gone on by now, and most definitely looking for him. Which Michael knew would make someone like Jimmy almost impossible to find.

Mike's phone lit up into life, from it's position on his bedside table. He removed it from it's charging cable, answering it. It was a young officer who had recently been seconded to the MIT. Mike had liked him, he seemed a good fit, but he'd thought that about Kate until yesterday. The officer PC Craig Potter, a 24 year old North Londoner. Craig had been raised with a silver spoon in his mouth, and as such didn't need to work, and was never going to be short of a few quid. This in Mike's mind made Craig harder to pay off, sure he could be wrong he wouldn't be the first man to succumb to the sin of greed, but Michael had noted Craig had always shown a strong work ethic.

It wasn't a long call, just a quick update. Craig knew he shouldn't be relaying information to Michael, and Mike had advised him of that, but Craig had stated Michael had taught him a lot during his tenure in MIT, and he felt he owed Mike a lot more than this phone call could offer.

PC Potter had found the Shawcross case incredibly intriguing. The police had identified all three bodies found at the property and located a murder weapon of one. The evidence, according to DCI Langford, pointed to Paul Shawcross. However, this didn't sit right with Craig, he could accept Shawcross being responsible for one murder, but having been at the murder scene he couldn't match it to the DCI's conclusion of the events.

Craig agreed the body they had identified as one Raymond Valentine, had in fact been murdered by Mr Shawcross. The other two victims however, had been identified as Mr Frank Price, and a Mr Harry Ward, both being employees of Mr Shawcross. They're murders, if committed by this Shawcross fella, would make no sense. From what Craig had seen, and Mike couldn't fault his thinking, Ward and Price seemed to be in the middle of disposing, of Mr Valentine's corpse when a third party had murdered them.

The DCI had shrugged this off, and simply stated if that had been the case there would have in fact been a fourth body, the lack of which, along with Shawcross' disappearing act, as well as a lack of any other suspect, had in Langford's mind, condemned PC Potter's deduction null and void.

Michael agreed, and at one point stated.

"That twat Langford couldn't detect a motor on the M25, during fucking rush hour!" Potentially over stepping the line ever so slightly. He also didn't really mean it he was still very pissed at his suspension. He also agreed with Craig's suggestion, that if they could find someone connected to Ray, they could solve this case.

Craig informed Michael he had drawn the short straw and had to inform the next of kin. This interested Mike as if they had next of kin, they would have an address, and for Michael that was enough to go on. This Ray must have been connected to Jimmy and what he was currently up to. He agreed to meet Craig at the Occasional Half public house in an hour. To provide support, in an unofficial capacity of course. He had just been suspended after all.

Chapter 43

It had proven to be a difficult morning for Marcus. Having to explain to Gregor how the Denim twins had proven too much, for a number of their best operatives. Gregor had been a lot more nonchalant than Marcus had expected. It was the first time Marcus had doubted his boss, in the forty odd years they'd worked together.

Marcus was infuriated, they're distribution had taken a massive hit. Krueger himself had been left with a large amount of product, in his possession that was quickly becoming unshift able. Not to mention with his clear foul mood, his house staff had been attempting to give him as wide a birth as they possibly could.

He had however contacted the Irishman, who in turn had jumped at the chance at another crack at Jimmy Denim.

"Yes, just don't fuck it up this time!" Krueger had warned him. The Irishman had argued his innocence, and how the last attempt hadn't been his fault.

"That's none of my concern!" Stated Marcus in his strong German accent. Another piece of luck presented itself, during the discussion with Gregor. Where Gregor had explained how he knew exactly where Jimmy would be, at some point that day. Information Marcus had passed on to the Irishman!

"And what about the Priest?" The Irishman had asked finally, Marcus had pondered this same question, and was very clear on what had to be done.

"Leave the Priest to me!" was all Krueger said before sitting back in his armchair, sparking a large Cuban cigar, and sipping at his glass of whisky.

Chapter 44

It was still early when Michael met Craig, outside the Occasional Half. The doors were still closed. Craig dressed in full uniform, holding his hat under his right arm. The uniform did little for him, at 5ft 6 it just made him look bulkier. Mie had always thought Craig looked far too young to be a copper. With his short, spiked hair, he looked like a 15-year-old schoolboy. They exchanged pleasantries, before approaching the door, giving it a curt knock, short loud but enough to grab the attention of those inside.

There came a shout from inside, it was a young lady.

"We're closed, come back at eleven!" Craig looked at Michael, looking for approval, Mike gave it with a simple nod.

"Sorry Miss, it's the police." Craig called at the window. They heard bolts slip down, and across, as the door opened slowly. A beautiful blonde-haired girl poked her head out.

"I'm sorry, can I help at all?" The young lady asked.

"Are you Miss Carly Valentine?" Craig asked, a bit too authoritatively for Michael's liking.

"Yes, is there something wrong?" Carly asked looking at Mike with a look of confusion.

"I'm sorry Miss, I'm DS Michael Denim, and this is PC Craig Potter. Would you mind if we come in, for a quick chat?" Michael requested in a much more sympathetic tone.

Carly invited them in, making sure to bolt the door behind them. She didn't want any regulars walking in on this. Ali then chose that moment to poke his head around the back room.

"Everything OK Carly?" He called out, spotting Mike walking through the bar. He cursed as Mike gave him an accusatory look. Craig took a step back, as Ali filled the bar with his hulking frame.

"Ali's fine PC Potter. What are you doing here though Ali?" Michael stated then asked.

"I'm looking after this one and Lacey. Ali replied smiling at Potter enjoying the moment of fear.

"What Lacey's here? Where's Jim?" Michael asked confused by this setup. If they were all here, they must have all known about Ray's murder.

"Jim's chasing a few leads. Gave me babysitting duties after yesterday." Ali stated, alluding to Liz's death.

"I don't believe that's why you're here though is it?" Ali continued with a question of his own, confirming Mike's suspicions. Michael looked at PC Potter, who had a look of suspicion on his face.

Ali eventually left the room, to check on Lacey. Carly sat at a table and invited the two police officers to join her. Potter did most of the talking, taking his time to explain how the police, had discovered her father's body. There were tears, plenty of questions. It became apparent to Michael and Carly that Potter, was already convinced of Jimmy's involvement. Michael couldn't workout how he'd become so convinced. Then Craig started asking specifically where Jimmy and Shawcross were and becoming increasingly aggressive with his questioning.

Michael started to feel uncomfortable. Potter was crossing the line now.

"I think you already knew about your father's death, didn't you?" Craig asked Carly staring directly into her eyes. She broke down again, then Ali appeared behind the door.

"OI, do you fucking mind? I've got an eight-year-old girl out here! Who don't need to hear all this!" Ali stated, Craig looked up at him.

"Who do you think your talking too." Craig glared at Ali now, all the fear from earlier had completely dissipated.

"You, now I think it's best you leave Officer!" Ali requested as politely as he could manage. Craig jumped up from his seat unzipping his stab vest, revealing the handle of a Browning 9mm. As he pulled the concealed weapon, from its hiding place Ali dove down behind the bar. Michael was closer but couldn't believe what was happening. The shock only lasted a split second before instinct kicked in.

As Craig took aim at Carly, Michael dived at Craig. Mike landed a rugby tackle, and the gun went off as they hit the floor. The Browning fell from Craig's grasp and slid across the pub floor. Michael made a grab for Craig's wrist, but he was too quick and planted a headbutt on Mike's nose. Unfortunately for PC Potter, he wasn't fast enough to avoid Ali's grasp!

Ali appeared from behind the bar, on Craig's blindside, just in time to see Mike wrestling with him. Ali closed the gap as Craig landed his headbutt. As Potter tried to press his advantage on DS Denim, Ali wrapped his right hand around the back of Potter's neck. Lifting him into the air and slamming a huge left hand under Craig's ribs. As soon as Ali released his grip it was clear the young PC had, had enough as he dropped to his knees.

Potter felt his legs buckle as his feet hit the floor. He was still struggling to catch his breath. When Mike swung a barstool at his head. Craig dropped as his world turned black, and he was swallowed by unconsciousness.

Chapter 45

I walked to my ex-father-in-law's house. I had borrowed a high collared jacket, which I had done all the way up, and a baseball cap from Carly. Walking with my head down would make me hard to pick out, even for the police facial recognition tech, I hoped.

As I approached the house Liz had grown up in, I decided to do a recon lap. It proved the right decision as I spotted two police cars on the road parked near the house I was after. I noted only one of the cars were marked, and empty. The officers must already be inside. The other car was an unmarked Astra, occupied by two smartly dressed male officers. I kept my distance, deciding to approach the rear of the property. I would watch any meeting between the plods and Arthur Cooper, from his bush lined garden.

One way or another, I knew I needed to talk to Arthur. The rear of the property was clear of any police presence, and luck was on my side. I could see Arthur, through the kitchen window. He had his head bowed, and was clearly weeping, whilst he was sat on a stool, beside his kitchen island. I saw a uniformed officer pass a box of tissues.

I watched for about half hour, before the police finally left. I climbed over the fence making my way down the right side of the back garden, staying out of view of the kitchen window. I knew the doors would be unlocked, it was mid-day and Arthur was home.

As I reached the back door, I placed a reassuring hand on my Gloch tucked into the back of my waistband. Without announcing my presence, I walked through the house, looking for Arthur. The house was immaculately kept. It always had been despite Arthur's wife dying almost two decades ago. The hallway was adorned with potted plants, and paintings. I found Arthur sat in his living room, drinking whisky and smoking a cigarette he was visibly distressed. I was about to add to his problems.

I walked in casually.

"Hello Arthur." I said nonchalantly. He looked round a look of shock, fear and dread, written on his weathered face. Arthur was in his mid-60s and could see the discussion with the police had aged him 10 years.

"Where the fuck did you come from?!" Arthur shouted; half screamed. I gave him a second to calm the fuck down.

"Wherever it is you can fuck right off back there!" He stated getting visibly agitated. To be fair we'd never had a great relationship. I had never been good enough for Arthur's little girl. Add to that he'd just found out he'd just lost said little girl. To a horrendously violent act, and now I waltzed into his home.

"I'm sorry about Liz." I offered my condolences.

"Your fucking sorry?! You jumped up little cunt! It should have been you!" He hissed his voice dripping with distain. That was when I lost it. I smashed the back of my hand, across his face. I dragged him up out his chair.

"Now you listen to me! This has probably got more to do with you, than it has me!" I told him through gritted teeth. I realised, with his reaction, that I'd hit the nail on the head. Although Arthur still had a bit of fight left in him.

"Don't you dare put this on me! You knocked the fucking hornet's nest; you couldn't leave shit alone. Now my little girls gone!" He informed me. The revelation that knew what I'd been doing, shocked me a little. It did however bring me nicely to the point of my visit. I pushed him back into his chair. I thought it would be best to change tact.

I walked past him, towards his drinks cabinet, pouring myself a whisky.

"Who the fuck do you think you are!" Arthur exclaimed with rightful indignation. I smiled back, taking a sip of whisky.

"I want you to listen to me now Arthur. I know your involved with these bastards." He tried to argue.

"I suppose your pal Ray told you all this!" It was a statement not a question.

"Actually, it was your mate, Shawcross." I told him.

"And from what I've seen your mates will kill you whether you talk or not!" I continued.

"You mean nothing to them. You owe them nothing, they sent the Priest after your fucking daughter for fuck's sake, Arthur helps me, bring them down!" I was close to begging and would have done if it would've helped. The last thing I wanted was to rob my daughter of her sole grandparent, a day after we'd lost her mother.

As we spoke a group photo, that I hadn't seen before. I only noticed it because I recognised Paulie. I also knew I hadn't seen it before for the same reason.

"Who the fuck are these people?" I asked. I spotted a flash from across the road, in the reflection of the photo frame. I dropped to the floor, screaming at Arthur to get down. I was too late. I saw blood forming in the middle of Arthur's chest. I crawled quickly across the floor, ducking behind the door, I felt a burn across the back of my thigh. As the bullet slid over it. I fucking hate snipers!

Chapter 46

Michael and Ali lifted P.C Potter into a chair using his own handcuffs to secure him in place. Carly went through to watch Lacey. As Michael attempted to argue with Ali, about proper police procedure.

"Look Mike, I couldn't give a monkey's toss, about police procedure! I ain't a copper, and this cunt certainly, didn't give two fucks, about proper police procedure, when he was trying to blow my fucking head off!" Ali made his colourful point.

It took a while for P.C Potter to regain consciousness. When he did, he wished he hadn't. The suspended D.S Denim, left the bar, accepting he was in enough trouble as it was. Although he couldn't help but listen to what was said, from behind the door.

"Right so who the fuck do you work for?" Ali asked looking over the gun P.C Potter had tried to kill them with.

"I'm a police officer, so her Majesty the Queen!" Craig answered sarcastically. Ali took a bottle of beer from behind the bar.

"I don't want to hurt you, but I don't want to wait for Jimmy to come back and find you here. Cause he will fuckin' hurt you." Ali informed him taking a swig of lager. Craig's eyes widened at the mention of the far more violent Denim twin. Ali found his mouth twist into a malicious smile. He was beginning to enjoy this more than he had expected. Ali had always prided himself on his hatred of bullies, and he tried to remind himself of that, but something kept pointing out that whoever Craig Potter worked for, were going to be the biggest bullies Ali had ever come across.

"Do what you like, I ain't tellin' you a god damn thing!" Craig stated defiantly.

Ali downed the last of the beer bottle and smashed the empty on a table. Before Ali made his move towards Craig, Michael re-entered the bar.

"Stand down Ali. I think P.C Potter and I need a chat. Officer to officer I think Craig owes me an explanation." Michael stated.

"You ain't a copper anymore Denim, won't be long now till you get done, for what you did to poor Kate." Came

Potter's response. Michael struck him the back of his right hand.

"What the fuck do you mean by that?" Mike was fuming.

"You know what that means, either you die, or you get sent down for so long, you'll wish you fucking died!" Potter answered laughing.

Chapter 47

I sat behind Arthur's front room door, for what seemed like an age. I needed that photo; Arthur always wrote names and dates on the backs of pictures. I may not have got any answers from Arthur, but I could well get something to go on. That was of course, if I survived this bastard sniper.

Suddenly I heard the tell-tale pop, of the sniper's silenced rifle. There was no shattered glass, this time. It appeared my friend had changed targets, which meant the police were about to gain entry. I had to move fast. I dived across the room towards Arthur's framed photograph collection. Another pop sounded, this time there was a crack of splintered glass. I felt the bullet burn, across my right arse cheek. The cunt was playing with me!

I gripped the framed image, and shuffled round, hiding behind a supporting wall. I knew I had to get out fast. My face would have been circulated across the Met's numerous officers by now and being caught here I'd be hard pressed to explain.

I heard another pop, again he was now clearly aiming at the police outside. It reminded me of an IRA ambush, me and Ali were caught in years ago, in South Armagh. Now I thought of it, I obtained a similar wound that day. Along with losing some bloody good blokes. I waited, I knew this bastard would be patient, but like me he couldn't wait forever. The arrival of a bigger police presence would have him scurrying off, like the ratty cunt he was. I wished I still had a flash bang with me. During the South Armagh incident, we'd used smoke grenades to cover our escape, I'd have killed for one just now.

Then came even worse news I heard sirens in the distance. I was definitely going to have to take a chance, death or incarceration. There was another pop from the rifle. It was now or never, I bolted around the corner, making for the front room door. The rifle fired again, taking more of Arthur's window. I dropped to a press up position, barely two feet from the cover of Arthur's hallway.

Another crack followed another shot. I leaped into the hallway, I felt the bullet strike the sole of my left boot, before slamming into the wall I'd left behind. I fell heavily into the hallway, jumping up and sprinting for the back entrance. I threw the back door open making good on my escape. I cleared Arthur's rear fence in one attempt. The pain in my arse increasing as the adrenaline wore off.

Once in the alleyway behind Arthur's house, I allowed myself a moment to calm down, catching my breathe walking casually as I could. I removed my jacket, tying it around my waist, obscuring any view of my bloody arse wound. The police were audibly drawing nearer. I kept my casual gait, the years had taught me, with the police bullshit baffles brains. If you look like you belong somewhere, nine times out of ten, the police will leave you alone, but if your busy doing your Linford Christie impression, you can guarantee getting your collar felt.

Before I reached the end of the alley, I removed the picture from it's frame, tossing the frame into a pile of bin bags. I pocketed the image. It was as I thought, Arthur had written names and a date on the back of the photograph. I didn't have to read them now. So, I continued my neutral looking stroll into the nearest Highstreet. Feeling staying public was my best bet. Hiding in plain sight and all that.

Chapter 48

Michael and Ali moved P.C Potter down to the beer cellar, so Carly could open the pub. They agreed, Ali would work the bar whilst Carly took Lacey into the back room. Mike then called Agent Daniels, he'd began trusting her more, considering what was happening with his own situation. She had informed Michael, her and Agent Fuller were on their way.

"Now your fucked. Those B.O.S 90 cunts have never heard of fuckin' proper procedure!" Michael advised Potter. The P. C's face dropped filling with fear.

"No, you've gotta let me out of here Denim! I'll tell you whatever you want to know. Just don't hand me over to them …. Mugs!" Craig laughed hysterically.

"You'll have to do better than that you cunt!" Potter said continuing to laugh. Mike punched him.

"I suggest you remain silent, you fucking bent slag!" Michael stated as he turned and headed upstairs. He didn't know how long the cavalry would be, but if he had to look at Potter much longer, there wouldn't be much left to question.

As Mike entered the bar area, Ali looked over, instantly grabbing a glass and heading for the optics, pouring a double measure of whisky.

"Here mate. You look as though you could do with it." Ali stated offering the glass.

"Yeah, I think I could." Mike responded knocking it back.

"Any word from Jim?" He continued.

"Nothing yet, he didn't even say who he was going to see. I think he's trying to distance us, from it all." Ali answered.

Ali poured two more doubles, necking one, and passing Michael the other.

"Anything out of that arsehole downstairs?" Ali asked.

"Not a fucking dickie bird." Was Mike's exasperated answer.

"I've got that MI5 pair coming down though. They should be able to get something, out of him." He finished, gulping down the whisky, enjoying the soft burn in his chest. Then they heard Potter's police radio crackle into life.

Reports of yet another shooting were coming through, with calls of officers down. Calls were coming in for urgent tactical response. Michael recognised the address immediately. Fear rushed over him, Jim was involved, if he'd started killing police officers, to hell with "a conflict of interest", and bollocks to "blood being thicker than water." If the armed response didn't take him down, then Michael fucking would. Reports of a sniper calmed Michael slightly, Jimmy was a few things, a sniper was not one of them.

The issue for now, was a strong need to be on scene helping, but he was suspended from active duty, and he couldn't leave Ali here with Potter, could he? There was a slight chance the MI5 Agents wouldn't make it to the pub for hours now.

Then two Eastern European men walked in. The first was short and dumpy, he was clearly in his early forties, and trying far too hard to reverse the effects of his age. His bleach blonde hair slicked back to cover the large bald spot, added to that was the poorly applied fake perma-tan. Wearing several gold rings, chains and thick cashmere coat. He looked like a Russian Del Boy. The other one made Michael tense; he was 7ft 10" with a massive muscular build. Wearing a grey Armani suit. Sporting a green mohawk sandwiched between two tattoos, a spider's web and a Chinese dragon. Even Ali took a step back as he soaked in the enormity of this giant. Something was wrong! Michael knew it, and so did Ali.

The Russians sat at a table, the short Russian beckoned for Michael, like he was some sort of waiter. Michael just stared at him.

"Bollocks to that!" Thought Mike. There was no way, Michael a D.S in the Met was offering this cunt a fucking table service.

"Yeah, what the fuck do you want?" Michael asked. The green haired monster's eyes narrowed. Blondie placed a gun on the table.

Chapter 49

I stopped into a corner shop, and bought 6 shot bottles of whiskey, then headed to a coffee shop further down the Highstreet. I ordered a cappuccino, pouring one of the bottles into it. I needed to work out my next move. I took Arthur's picture from my pocket. It was of five men, in golfing outfits. I could identify three without, looking at the names on the back, obviously I could see Arthur on the end, on the right-hand side. On the other end was both Paulie Shawcross, and John O'Grady. The other two men I didn't recognise, but good old Arthur had come through for me, naming the two strangers on the back of the photograph. The main looking one in the middle, was identified as Marcus Krueger, the other was Jonathon Priestly.

Krueger was a tall man with short blonde spiked hair, and really stood out. He was well built, where as Priestly was wiry, with long black hair. I'd just started piecing the information together, when a familiar face walked into the coffee shop. A woman in her mid-thirties, she'd been a friend of Liz's for several years. Her name was Felicity, but she had always preferred "Flick". Felicity was a very attractive woman, and very posh, I had on occasion wound Liz up, referring to Felicity as "Mrs Bouquet." Her hair was long blonde and feathered. Today, like most, she wore a tight floral dress, which accentuated her curves.

"Jimmy? Is that you?" She called out lowering her sunglasses. Before I could answer, she had already run over.

"I'm so sorry to hear your news." She stated.

"How did you know?" I asked confused, I hadn't told anyone, and I was sure the police wouldn't have thought to contact Felicity on my behalf. I didn't like her answer.

"You're all over the news Jim. It's fine I know you would never hurt Liz." She said smiling. I gave her a curt smile in response. Then it hit me, I was all over the news! That complicated things. I gathered as well, from Felicity's reassurance, I was now definitely wanted for murder!

I don't know how, but after that realisation, I managed to convince Felicity, to take me back to her place. Reasoning if I was wrongfully wanted for murder, a very public coffee shop, probably not the best place, for me to conduct my investigations. I played on it being much easier to clear my name there, than here. What ever it was, luckily Felicity accepted.

Chapter 50

Michael froze for a split second, when first confronted with the gun. The blonde Russian calmly rested his hand on the firearm, as his friend stood up offering Michael the seat, with a grunt.

"I'd rather not hurt you, D.S Denim! My colleague Rock on the other hand is hoping, you're feeling less than co-operative." Blondie stated, in a thick Russian accent.

Michael could feel Ali glaring at Rock, Ali looked at Rock and simply saw a true challenge. The two behemoths wouldn't take their eyes off each other, both longing to lock horns. Michael wished to air on the side of caution, whilst the gun was in play.

"Well, what do you want?" Mike asked the Russian.

"P.C Potter!" Was his simple heavily accented response. Michael was stunned. How did this bastard know Potter was here? Could he pass over another police officer, not when these two were definitely going to kill him if he did. Add to that it meant Potter knew more than he'd let on so far.

"Just take him out Vlad! I'll deal with Pee-Wee, and we can leave!" Demanded Rock. Ali leaped over the bar, but Vlad quickly, coolly lifted the pistol from the table. Ali froze barely two feet from Rock. Vlad didn't fire he simply sat in his chair; his firearm trained on Ali's chest.

"That's enough from you pair!" Vlad was clearly in control of the situation.

"Mr Denim, I want P.C Potter, it doesn't need to get messy. Unless you and your friend insist on complicating this simple transaction." Vlad reasoned.

Michael weighed up his options, and ultimately, they would result in risking his life to save Potter's, giving up his and Ali's lives inevitably ending with Potter losing his life soon after, or letting these two bastards kill Potter, and hoping they left without killing Mike, Ali, Carly and Lacey. As options went, they were some slim fucking pickings, Michael thought. Then he remembered the MI5 Agents were on their way, if he could stall these bastards long enough, there might be a chance for everyone to survive this.

"He's not here. He came with me to inform the landlord of a death, and then he went back to the station." Michael lied. Vlad looked him up and down, slowly, and purposefully moving the gun across to Michael's direction.

"That's not the answer I want, Mr Denim!" Vlad stated as his finger tensed on the trigger.

"If you lie to me again, I will shoot you! And then I will kill Mr Smith here, and I will follow that by killing Your niece and the lovely Miss Valentine out the back there." Shit, thought Mike, this cunt's intel was on point.

"Fuck! OK, he's down in the cellar. Take him and fuck off." Mike said defeated. He could risk his life, shit he did on a daily basis, but he couldn't risk Lacey's. Vlad lowered the pistol and nodded in Rock's direction. As Rock made his way down to the basement, Michael prayed that the MI5 Agents would hurry up and walk through the door. They didn't, but Mike just kept praying.

Chapter 51

We made it to Felicity's riverside penthouse apartment, at about mid-day. It was a beautiful one bed place. It was a very modernly decorated, all the furniture was either leather, or glass. What furniture there was, I think the term was minimalist. The living room area was huge, with large glass doors overlooking the river, two black leather sofas almost flanked a wall mounted TV.

Felicity instructed me to make myself at home, so I took a seat on the sofa, looking out the large glass doors, at the river. It was somewhat calming. Which I definitely needed today. Felicity appeared with two glasses of wine. I'd taken the time in the coffee shop, to patch my arse wound, so I was happy I wasn't getting blood all over Felicity's sofa. Felicity passed one glass in my direction, I thanked her and took a sip.

"So, what do you know about Liz, so far?" She asked softly. I looked at her, trying to think how much I should share with her. I wasn't sure but opted to share what I knew, whilst keeping my parent's and therefore mostly my own involvement quiet for the time being.

"After seeing her, I'm convinced it's this Priest fella." I told her.

"But why Liz? That's what I don't understand." Felicity asked, obviously it was a warning to me, just as the attack on Carly had been for Ray.

Suddenly the mood changed, I started to notice the change in her behaviour. She started stroking the top of her thigh, whilst staring at me intently.

"I'll never understand what Liz did to you!" Felicity stated.

"I mean that Warren was a step down really." She added as she leaned over, placing a hand on my leg. I reached for my wine glass, subtly brushing her hand away. As I polished off the wine, I began thinking now was the time to get back to the pub. As I stood up to say as much, I realised something was very wrong.

My head was suddenly swimming, as I fell back on the sofa, Felicity swung round so we were face to face. She was smiling as she ran her hands down my chest. I couldn't argue, as my arms and legs began to numb.

"Oh Jim, I'm sorry, it looks like the wines gone to your head, let me help you into bed." She said a wicked smile on her face. I slumped further into the sofa as the room began to spin, then grow black as I slipped into unconsciousness.

Chapter 52

Ali maintained a hard stare, watching Vlad, waiting for an opportunity. He was also aware of any sign of movement out of the back of the bar. Rock hadn't been more than a minute. Ali knew he would only get a short window, to wrestle control of this situation. A quick glance at Michael confirmed he was thinking the same.

Ali ran his hand over the bar, intentionally knocking a nearby stella glass. The smash that followed drew Vlad's attention, buying Michael a moment. Michael didn't need a second invitation. He knew this would be their best chance of survival. He lunged at Vlad grabbing his gun arm and launching his knee into Vlad's gut. Vlad let out a primal cry, as the gun fired.

The bullet stuck one of the optics behind the bar. Ali dove over the bar, trying to ensure Vlad was suitably subdued, but the gun went off a second time, as Michael wrestled Vlad to the floor. The two of them froze as soon as the shot was discharged.

Ali, almost comedically, patted himself down almost looking for a hole, there wasn't one. He thanked God, then he heard Rock running through to the bar, he was barking questions.

"What the fuck is going on Vlad?" He called.

"The bastard's already dead!?" Rock continued clearly confused.

Michael jumped up, now holding the gun. He trained it on Rock.

"Vlad's dead too." Michael stated, nonchalantly. Fixing Rock with a menacing glare.

"Now sit the fuck down, I've a few questions for you!" Michael finished.

Before Rock moved the pub door flung open.

"ARMED POLICE! DROP YOUR WEAPONS AND PLACE YOUR HANDS ON YOUR HEADS!" The leading officer screamed! As soon as Mike placed Vlad's gun on the floor, Rock spun and bolted for the door.

"Fuck." Michael exhaled, exhausted and knowing what was about to happen.

It wasn't long before the pub, was teaming with armed coppers. SOCO officers had arrived, along with the man Michael thought would be his soon to be, former boss. Michael knew what this looked like. He couldn't argue, he'd definitely killed Vlad, thankfully Ali would be a witness for self-defence, but they both heard Rock.

"The bastard's already dead." He must have meant Potter, and they couldn't explain why he'd been tied up in a pub basement. Michael also knew the bent copper statement, however true, would soon come under serious scrutiny. It did however appear at this moment in the time half the fucking force was bent!

Chapter 53

I don't know how long I was out for, but when I did regain consciousness, I was filled with dread. My whole body was racked with pain. My head was pounding, and I had a massive pressure on my shoulders. It took me a few seconds to take in my surroundings, and realise the fact I was naked, and hanging from my chained wrists, on what looked like a meat hook. It took me a little longer still, to register I wasn't alone.

There were currently three of us, in the dark dank basement. The only light coming from a decrepit florescent bulb, which only added to my growing headache. I had to work hard to focus, and when I did, it looked like we were in a serial killer's personal playhouse. The floor, which sat inches from my feet's reach, was covered in a clear plastic sheeting. There were two small almost surgical tables, one just in front of me, laid out with a scalpel and a large hunting knife. I tried adjusting my weight to try and alleviate the stress on my shoulders, as I peered over to my right.

I heard her scream, as my eyes locked on to her. It was Felicity, and she was in the same predicament as me. Naked and hanging from the basement ceiling, her hands bound in chains dangling inches from the floor, on the end of a large meat hook. Her slender naked frame covered in tiny cuts. Then my gaze locked onto the man with the knife, and I knew instantly this was the bastard I'd been looking for! This was the twisted cunt who'd murdered Liz, and all those poor kids, who'd attempted to rape and murder CJ. The man with the knife was the Priest!

Felicity's screams soon subsided, as the Priest put down the scalpel, they were replaced by sobs, and panicked questions, and pleading statements. I found myself feeling very sorry for her, allowing myself the opportunity to forget how screwed we both were. Then Felicity said something, and with that one sentence she reignited my rage at recent events.

"Marcus won't allow you to get away with this!" Felicity stated with a sense of confidence that belittled her inevitable fate, but the confidence ebbed away just as quickly as it had arisen.

"I delivered sleeping beauty over there!" This time she sounded almost hysterical. That was when I realised, that bitch had sold me out! My concern was extinguished there and then. We were both going to die, and it was entirely her fault!

Felicity didn't get to argue anymore, I watched as the Priest ran a gloved hand across the large hunting knife, finally resting his hand on the hilt of the blade. Then in one swift movement, he spun jabbing the knife into Felicity's throat. My stomach lurched at the sound of her gurgled pleas, as her life leaked through the open wound. He lowered Felicity's corpse onto the floor, before kneeling across her chest, and drew his blade down her neck, this time carving a line down, making the initial wound look like a crucifix.

Then the sense of dread returned, washing over me in waves, as he stood and focused all his attention in my direction.

"Ah, at last you're awake Mr Denim, I've been looking forward to seeing you again." He informed me, making no effort to disguise the malice in his voice. I simply stared at him, refusing to show any fear, this bastard would only get off on it. I knew however I needed to turn this around, but that would start by getting on the fucking floor!

Chapter 54

"What the fuck is fucking wrong with you Denim?!" DCI Langford raged, his face a hot red and his eyes bulging.

"I'm sure I told you to leave this alone, now here you are with two more bleeding corpses!" Michael didn't have an answer, not one Langford would like anyway. Fortunately for Michael and Ali it had soon become apparent they were not responsible for Potter's death. Although it still didn't look good being in this close proximity to a murder and not being able to provide any information.

It appeared now that Potter had been killed by the Priest. It hadn't taken long after the arrival of Daniels and Fuller, for them to turn the place over, looking for any sliver of evidence that could finally ID the Priest, but as usual there was nothing. Ali and Michael were clear of any charges in regard to Vlad, but there were still questions to answer, as to what PC Potter had been doing in the pub, not to mention why he was dead, tied to a chair in the pub cellar. Luckily with Vlad's presence there was enough doubt and lack of evidence to give either man as much as a reprimand. That wouldn't stop Langford, from giving Michael the third degree, nor stop him reading Mike a very detailed riot act.

All in all, it could've been a lot worse, Michael thought as the police continued gathering forensics. Daniels and Fuller insisted taking Michael, Ali, CJ and Lacey into protective custody. Ali wasn't happy about it, but in the end had to accept they didn't have a lot of choice in the matter, and there was far too many old Bill about to argue.

The pub now would be closed, for the entirety of the police investigation. Ali and CJ both tried covertly to text Jimmy warning to stay clear, whether he'd received the intel in time was anyone's guess, having not updated anyone on his progressor lack of.

Chapter 55

The Priest stood staring at me, for a long time before he spoke again.

"You know Jim, it's almost a shame to kill you like this, all trussed up, you've proven quite the worthy adversary. I genuinely thought you were going to kill me in the pub." He said calmly picking up a scalpel, and eye-bawling the stitching across my chest.

My stomach lurched again, as he slowly raised the scalpel to my wound, before drawing it across the stitches. It wasn't as painful as I'd expected, although it felt strange as the skin separated again. Then he exploded into a flurry of swipes, the pain was shocking, the blade hit several times. I felt the blood trickle from my fresh wounds.

"Cunt!" I grunted unintentionally, he simply smiled under that fucking clear mask. I knew the bastard was going to get off on any reaction I gave him.

"It's so disappointing not have your daughter here, with us. I would have loved to have seen you face as I carved her up in front of you!" Hissed the killer. I snapped lashing out with a leg landing a snappy kick on the underside of his jaw. It knocked him back, whilst causing my shoulders to carry more weight. His head spun his face had a clear look of malice under his fucking mask.

"That's going to fucking cost you, you stupid prick!" He lashed out again with his scalpel. The flurry this time was very accurate, slicing into muscle whilst avoiding main arteries, whilst hitting spots that would bleed and hurt. I felt the blade slice just under my arm pit.

Then a ringing sound burst into life, from behind the cellar door. I welcomed the distraction etched on the Priest's face, under that bastard mask!

"Hold tight treacle. I won't be long." He informed me, as he left the room. I knew this could be my last opportunity! I tried to take in all of my surroundings trying desperately to find a way out of my bindings.

In the end I used the restraints to lift myself up and down a few times, trying to get some feeling back in my arms. It caused more blood to seep down my arms. That was when I looked up at the meat hook above me. I knew I was taking too long, but I didn't know what to do. The adrenaline was coursing through my blood. It was clouding my judgment causing me to rush my decisions. Panic was setting in, as I realised the bastard could be back with me at any point.

I tried to swing myself free, but I couldn't get the chains over the tip of the hook. I raised my legs up to the ceiling, using my knees to grip the chain above the meat hook. Then I was able to ease my hands over the hook. Fear surged through me as my knees started to slide down the chain. If I came down too quickly, I could impale myself on the hook and then I'd definitely be dead. It only got worse as I could now hear the bastard moving around with doors closing.

My hands were clammy with sweat. Somehow, I managed to lower myself slowly. Easing myself down before dropping the few inches on to the plastic coverall on the floor.

This was it now, when the Priest came back down here, I'd kill him, or die trying!

I crept across the room, ducking down just out of view, and next to the door. I could hear him talking to someone he called Marcus.

"Yes, Marcus that's what I said, I have him! Yes, she's already been dealt with, I'm about to finish him now!" He stated. It had to be Marcus Krueger, from Arthur's photograph, once I got out of here that bastard was next! I strained waiting, trying to hear as much of the conversation as I could, any blanks I'd have to force out of the Priest before I ended him. Then I heard it.

"Look if Gregor trusts in my abilities, why the fuck can't you?" Yelled the Priest. A name, and the that was said, would imply this Gregor was above Marcus.

Then came my moment. I heard him slam down the receiver, blurt out a few expletives and throw the cellar door open.

"What the fuck?" He stood in the doorway, confused by the empty hook, where he'd had me hanging helpless just moments before. He stomped down the stairs.

"Come out now then, don't be a coward!" He demanded, but I was already behind him. I threw my wrist restraints over his head, using the chains like a garrot wire. He flailed about knowing I had him bang to rights now. I struggled to keep hold of him as he tried to fight back. Every blow risked my grip.

Slowly the blows decreased in speed and power. Just before he lost consciousness I released him, pushing him across the room. He slowly got to his feet, coughing and spluttering, trying to catch his breath. I didn't give him chance to gather himself completely, I wrapped the chains around my hands, and smashed them into his head as hard as I could. He fell to the floor heavily.

I checked his pockets, eventually finding his keys. I released my hands, then put the restraints on his wrists, fixing him to a metal pipe fixed to the wall. I grabbed the large hunting knife and waited for him to wake up. Although I could be in for a long wait, I hit him pretty fucking hard.

Chapter 56

The Irishman sat in the shitty hotel room, Klichkov had put him up in. He lit a smoke and poured a whisky. Today had been a bad day. In fact, every day he had heard the name Denim, had been a bad day these last few years, maybe he was getting to old for this line of work, he had more than enough money to disappear, to some tropical island somewhere, and live out the rest of his days in peace and tranquillity, but he couldn't, no not yet, not while that prick Denim was still breathing.

Four times now that little bastard had slipped through his fingers, the Irishman thought taking a long drag on his cigarette. He never failed to kill his targets, NEVER! He drained his glass of whisky, feeling the satisfying burn of the liquor in his gut rising up into his lungs. This bastard Denim seemed to have the "luck of the Irish" the irony not lost on the agitated Irishman. He turned on the poxy 24-inch TV, which sat on a shelf at the foot of the bed and tried to recall each time he had Denim's fate in his hands. When the Irishman had him in his sights, bang to rights. If he could remember where he'd gone wrong each time before maybe, just maybe, Denim's luck would finally run out!

He poured another whisky, took another long drag of his fag, and thought back to that day, in the mountain range of Zagros in Iraq. It had been a long day; the sun and heat had been unrelenting. He had tracked his target's unit to their over night camp site. As they set up their bivvies, about mid-way up one of the mountains, they appeared to also be on their own hunt. The Irishman hunted down a spot of high ground overlooking the small band of British soldiers. The killer had set up his own poncho, and sniper's rifle. He was ready, and as usual his quarry wouldn't even see him coming.

He watched as the squaddies readied their meals on their Hexi stoves. Suddenly something caught the Irishman's eye, just 10 yards from the biggest soldier, was an IED, then he noticed one of the idiots heading straight for it! He dropped to a firing position, reattaching his scope to the rifle, not sure what to do, he could shoot the IED, but he'd give away the element of surprise, or he could kill Denim, take his chances with the rest of the squad. Ultimately, he would always choose to kill the Denim boy, even if he hadn't had chance to evaluate the others in the group.

Then as Private Jimmy Denim's face filled the Irishman's rifle scope, and his finger slowly tensed on the trigger, a shot rang out, and the IED exploded. The blast engulfed the young paratrooper, shards of metal flew through the air. The giant trooper howled in pain, as chunks of metal ripped through his legs, and in that split second, the Irishman's attention was divided. On top of this distraction the area was now filled with black acrid smoke, and with that the opportunity had passed. The unit were now mobilising, dealing with the wounded. It wouldn't be long until they located the Irishman. He had lost out on Denim through bad fucking luck!

It didn't take long for the Irishman to find, the soppy cunt, behind the IED. It had been a young native fella, Ahmed Massa. Ahmed had spent a day bragging to as many locals as he could, all about his exploits, and how he had evaded capture from the great British paratrooper regiment. He didn't evade the Irishman, however. As Ahmed left the local Mosque the Irishman had caught him. Cutting his throat from ear to ear and enjoying watching the life fade from the boy's eyes.

The Irishman downed and refilled his whisky. Taking another long drag, the memory of killing Massa making him feel better. Then his burner phone sprang to life. It would be his employer, or Klichkov, the Irishman's financial benefactor. He answered, the German accent gave his ID, his employer, Krueger was a harsh man, and he was calling the Irishman off, he'd been beaten to Denim by that bastard nonce, The Priest, but not all was lost, as Krueger gave him his latest target. His new target was the Priest.

The Irishman inhaled the last of his cigarette, before stubbing it out. He was going to enjoy killing the Priest. It made a change to kill someone who 100% deserved it, and no one deserved it more than the Priest.

Chapter 57

I located my belongings upstairs, after leaving the cellar. The Priest, it appeared, was an actual priest, his house was adorned with several religious items. It made me hate the cunt even more! It was bad enough that I knew men were capable of the crimes this bastard had committed, but a man of the cloth, the idea both infuriated, and disgusted me. After finding my belongings I was at least thankful my Gloch was untouched, after giving it a quick check, and replacing the safety, I placed it in my waistband, and headed down to the Priest.

I allowed myself a wry smile, as I entered the cellar, and saw the Priest, furiously trying to free himself.

"You want to struggle, you horrible cunt!" I told him, still wearing my smile. I pulled my gun from my waistband, making a point of letting him see it before I placed it on the table. I knelt down so I level with him.

"I'm not going to lie to you. I'm going to kill you, whether you answer my questions, or not, but if you do answer them, I'll make it quick. If not, and I fucking hope you don't, I'll drag it out, and believe me, I want to fucking hurt you!" I told him. He gave me a defiant stare, I double jabbed him nose and mouth, breaking his nose. He called me something I thought it was cunt, but I couldn't make it out through his mouthful of claret. I stood him up and kicked him in the lower ribs.

"First ones nice and easy. I assume this kill room of yours is soundproof, isn't it?" I asked, knowing he wouldn't be stupid enough to do what he did, without making sure his victims couldn't be heard. Again, he simply stared at me, the contempt evident in his eyes. I picked up a scalpel and ran the blade over the top of his right collar bone. He smirked.

"I've been cutting myself since I was a fucking child! You fucking amateur!" He scolded me. I smiled back, then forced my fingers into the wound, deep enough to grip the bone. His eyes widened, and this time he let out a primal scream, filled with pain.

"Fucking amateur!" I mocked.

"I'll come back to that and snap it!" I added.

I had wanted to rip it clean from his chest, but that would've sent him into shock, and he'd be no good to anyone. As much pain as I wanted to inflict on this cunt, it had to be administered gradually.

"Of course, it's fucking soundproofed! You sadistic cunt!" He screamed, I simply smiled watching the tears stream down his face. I picked up my Gloch and rested the barrel on his left knee.

"Who the fuck is Marcus?" I asked, he wriggled uncomfortably in his restraints, knowing what was about to happen. In the end he hesitated too long for my patience. I pulled the trigger, blood, cartilage, and bone leaped from the hole left by my bullet. I wiped a few bloodied bone fragments from my face and moved my gun to his other knee.

"Who the FUCK is Marcus?" I repeated my question through his scream. This time he didn't hesitate.

"He's, her husband!" He informed me through short breaths, trying to alleviate some of the pain it wouldn't work, as I shoved my finger into the wound. Just to keep him honest.

It was almost liberating not having to rush my questions. The Priest had made time, and witness' redundant. The serial killer's property was perfect for torturing and murdering this piece of shit.

Unfortunately, for the Priest, I'm not a very patient person, with every hesitation came another bullet. The pain would've been immense, at least the Priest made it seem unbearable. The cellar was covered in blood, bone, muscle and cartilage, but a story was beginning to form. He gave me names, and seemed to know a few details, but didn't know the name of my parents' shooter.

According to the Priest, my father had been invited to join a criminal organisation, after coming to their attention for his work with my grandfather. I had to say I was learning more about my family history this week than in the last 37 years. My Mother was the daughter of a mafia Don, who had adopted my father and Aunt. I took pride from the knowledge my father had knocked back their offer, due to their support of paedophile rings, and people trafficking.

His refusal had led to the head of the organisation a Gregor Klichkov, made the decision to have his whole family executed. The only information the Priest could offer on the triggerman, however, was that he was Irish, so only a couple of million leads to go on there. I always found it amusing how talkative people got with a few bullet holes in them. Especially when they were put in specific places, where they wouldn't hit any vital organs.

That being said, I could see the Priest was fading. His skin was now nearly grey in colour. His eyes started to roll into the back of his head, and his answers were becoming more, and more incoherent. It was almost time to end this. The pain racked through my body, due to all the battle wounds, I'd accumulated through out the last few days. I placed the gun on the table and retrieved the large hunting knife.

I knelt down again, staring into the Priest's eyes.

"Well looks like we're done here then." I informed him calmly, there was a callousness to my voice.

"Just fucking do it!" He snapped, ready to finally die. I nodded and slowly inserted the blade into his chest. It was over in seconds, and without a struggle. It was I thought a bit anti-climactic. Would the others feel like this? No real sense of justice finally being served. had I gone about this all in the wrong way? It was only now hitting me, maybe these bastards should be dying in prison, not in their luxurious homes. No, I couldn't think like that. The police had, had decades to catch these cunts, and enforce punishment upon them. No justice would never be served on criminals like these. These bastards deserved vengeance! Nothing more, nothing less!

Still, I found myself, fishing in my pocket for my mobile phone. I scrolled down to Kate's number, at this point she'd be easier to talk to than Mike, and that meant I might stay out of jail, until at least I'd had a shot at the bastards behind my parents' murders. As if I could be that lucky. It answered on the second ring, but not by Kate, but by an older male voice.

"DCI Langford! DC Kate Marshall's phone?" His booming voice filled my ear. I had to think fast, the DCI was definitely the last person I needed to be talking to.

"Where's Kate?" I asked sternly, hoping he wouldn't ask who I was. As usual I wasn't that lucky.

I fobbed him off with a false ID claiming to be Kate's boyfriend. That was when he dropped the news, that Kate had died in a RTC yesterday.

"What about her partner?" I asked, the pain, anguish and concern evident in my voice.

"Michael's fine, Jimmy." He informed me, emotionlessly.

"Kate's phone has caller ID, and you need to hand yourself in! You're in a shit ton of trouble!" He'd been playing me the whole time. The fucking arsehole! I hung up refusing to get into a discussion about my recent wrongdoing.

I had to bite the bullet! I scrolled through to Mike's number, I paused for a long time before pressing to activate the call.

Chapter 58

DCI Langford threw Kate's phone across his office.

"Who the fuck do these Denim cunts think they are!" He thought. He was still raging at Kate's death. She'd been a great prospect, as well as an amazing fuck. At least they'd covered their backs. Normally an office affair between a DCI and a DC would have been the talk of the force, with both of them being reprimanded. Worse than that, they'd made a lot of money between them, that could stop now, it would be much harder covering his back without a partner.

He also now needed to inform the German, that Jimmy was in fact still FUCKING breathing. Which also meant chances were, the Priest was already dead. The DCI didn't mind that too much at least if he were dead those two cock suckers from MI5 would finally be out of his hair!

*   *   *

Marcus listened intently to Langford, as he whined down the phone. He often wondered, why the English always seemed to put such weak fools in positions of power? It often made his life easier, but for law abiding citizens, the UK was going to hell in a fucking handbag! The Priest had failed and was in all likelihood dead. Which Marcus thought was timely, the Priest had started to outlive his usefulness! A point proven as Denim had survived, unlike Krueger's wife. His wife, who had also outlived her purpose.

Fortunately, the Irishman was already on his way to the Priest's base of operations. Even if Krueger had started to doubt the Irishman's ability to keep up these days, he had to think this would be his best chance at finally taking Denim out!

*   *   *

Michael's phone started to belt out his ringtone, as the MI5 people carrier hurtled down the M2 coastbound. Agent Daniels fixed him with a hard stare.

"It's Jimmy." Mike informed her, as he looked at the screen.

"Well fucking answer, it!" She insisted, before turning to Fuller.

"Get a trace on that call! Mike answer that fucking phone and keep him on the line until we've got his location!" She finished her commands. Ali fixed Mike with a hard stare. CJ stayed quiet, just relieved to know Jimmy was OK.

It took Fuller 5 minutes to trace the call. Despite Jimmy, insisting they trace it, his phone signal kept dipping in and out. He tried to fill Mike in on his current situation, and how the Priest wouldn't be a problem anymore. Daniels glared at Mike.

"What the fuck does he mean by that?" She demanded an explanation.

"Probably that he's dead!" Ali answered.

"And fair play to him, I fucking say!" He added, Daniels glaring at him the whole time.

"Sorry treacle but should you not be watching the FUCKING road!" He finished, as she huffed, informing Fuller they were going to need a closer safehouse, to leave CJ and Lacey. Ali nudged CJ.

"Fucking women drivers like that, give the rest of you a bad fucking name." He told her with a wink, she chuckled nodding in agreement.

*   *   *

The Irishman's eyes had lit up, when #krueger had called with the news. The Priest had screwed the pooch, on the Denim boy, now he had another chance to finally slug that bastard Denim!

Chapter 59

I didn't enjoy the tone of that phone call, I liked Langford's even less. Worst of all those MI5 wankers insisted, I stay put, however I knew what a risk that was, now so many people were aware of my survival. Anyone could be on they're way here. If Krueger somehow found out I was alive, anyone could turn up, and considering the size of the criminal organisation I was up against, they absolutely had members of the police on their payroll.

Staying put was huge fucking risk. To both my life and my liberty. Deep down I knew it was a risk I had to take, I needed back up, and if I did run, I had absolutely no idea where I was. I sparked a smoke, and began searching the Priest's home for any alcohol, and or painkillers.

I located everything I needed in the kitchen, for my latest first aid needs. I swigged at a half full bottle of impressively expensive whisky, knocking back some fairly strong painkillers, before taping up my chest wound. I found some anti-septic, and cleaned up my other injuries, from the Priest's scalpel, as I waited for the back up or the police or ultimately my killer to arrive.

As I waited, I allowed my mind to recall my conversation with Michael. I began to realise I recognised the voice of the woman, who had been barking orders at my brother. I was positive the voice had belonged to Victoria Fuller. Sorry Flight Sergeant Victoria Fuller. A woman I had met in the mid 90's, whilst I was serving in the Paras, more accurately it was during my passing out parade.

It was back in 94 that I'd met William Fuller's sister. William was a well to do twat, and a fast-track Rupert. All of us recruits fucking hated the cunt. Passing out of training, and obtaining my red beret, as it was for everyone else to ever do it, was a huge achievement. Normally you had your whole family there to celebrate with you, but at the time I only had two people I could consider family. One was my twin brother Michael, the other was (my then fiancé) Angela.

We had sat at a table, in a small military bar (or NAFFI as we called it.) As with all military gatherings, copious amounts of alcohol were consumed. After an hour or so I noticed a young woman in full RAF uniform, looking in my direction, from the Fuller family's table. I had always had a thing for women in uniform, especially in the nineties. Women's uniforms in the 90's had a certain attractive class about them.

I knew my fiancé was there, but I'm sure I've stated, when I was young, I was somewhat of a bastard. I honestly have no idea why Angela ever put up with me. After a couple of looks and a bit of flirting at the bar, she made the invite. When the opportunity arose, we both made our excuses to our tables, and headed to the restrooms.

I followed Victoria out of the bar. She grabbed my green shirt, and pulled me into the ladies, kissing me hard. We stumbled into a cubicle, our hands all over each other's bodies. As I turned, from locking the door, she fixed me with lust filled eyes. We practically tore at each other's uniforms. I groped her impressively large breasts squeezing them together, as she fumbled with my belt. She grabbed my hard cock and slid down to her knees, enveloping my cock in her mouth. She felt amazing, but there wasn't time for that. I pulled away lifting her to her feet.

I spun her round and hitched up her skirt. I rubbed her pussy through her tight. I could feel her getting wetter under my touch. That's when I realised, she wasn't wearing any underwear, so I reached down and pulled hard at both sides of the crotch of her tights ripping a hole, revealing her wet pussy. Victoria let out a short gasp. She spun round and leaning over pushing her arse out and looking over her shoulder.

"Fuck me now!" She demanded; I grabbed the base of her ponytail as I eased my dick into her. I started slow, pulling her hair softly before speeding up my efforts. I felt one of her legs buckle, as she screamed out.

I pulled out, spinning her round to face me. I kissed her hard, forcing her back to the wall. I lifted her up by the waist, and she wrapped her legs around me, guiding my cock back inside her. This time I didn't ease my way, I simply picked up where I'd left off. Sliding in and out at furious pace. I felt the pressure building, she kissed me hard as I exploded inside her.

That was when she pushed me off, and fished a pair of black knickers, from her blazer pocket.

"Right now, wash up, and fuck off." She ordered as she pulled up her fresh panties, brushing down her uniform.

"Wouldn't want your fiancé working out what you've just done, do we?" She asked not expecting an answer as she left me, half dressed in the ladies toilets.

I did as I'd been ordered readjusting my uniform, before exiting the ladies. I saw William, and I'm a little ashamed to say a smirk spread across my face. He flew at me, screaming.

"YOU DIRTY BASTARD! YOU'RE A FUCKING DEADMAN!" He ranted, before landing a right hand on my chin. The hit made me stumble, I righted myself and looked William in the eye.

"Fucking so worth it." I'd stated and headed back to the bar.

That had been the last time I'd ever seen Victoria; I did have a few tours with William. When ever I did run into him, I always made sure to whined him up. Whether it was simply asking how Victoria was doing or occasionally something cruder.

I couldn't help but think how could Victoria Fuller be involved in all this? And what would that mean for me?

Chapter 60

There was a large, wooded area, next to the Priest's property, the afore mentioned wood spanned about a mile before being split by a poorly lit side road. This was where the Irishman had decided to park up (dump) the shit heap Fiesta he'd acquired an hour prior. He retrieved the holdall he'd dumped on the back seats. The trees offered the ideal cover for the Irishman's activities.

*   *   *

It took the MI5 Agents, along with Michael and Ali, about an hour to drop CJ and Lacey off at the safe house. It would take them a further hour from there to reach Jimmy's location.

There had been a few revelations on the way to the Priest's bolt hole. The first came when Ali refused to stay at the safehouse.

"I was in the Paras I ain't missing out on any of this!" Ali had stated. The MI5 Agents couldn't argue, nor would they want to. Michael was another issue he knew the ins and outs of the case and could be a huge help.

*   *   *

Langford knew he was in trouble as soon as he saw Rock stood outside his office. This was the problem with playing both sides. He breezed past Rock, trying desperately not to show any sign of fear. Showing Rock just how intimidating his size would be a serious mistake. Hiding the terror, he felt when he saw Klichkov sitting at his desk, was entirely redundant.

"I remember, when you were mere PC." Gregor spoke, freezing Langford to the spot.

"I think I prefer you then." The Russian mused.

"As PC you would do anything I ask, so eager to please." That was when Langford opted to grow a pair. He straightened his back and puffed out his chest.

"What are you doing here?" He asked.

"You could blow the entire operation; I've told you never to come here. And to show up with Bigfoot! You could throw my integrity into serious question! Then what good am I to you?" He'd made a mistake, nobody ever questioned Gregor Klichkov.

Klichkov reached into the top drawer, of Langford's desk retrieving a cheap bottle of whisky.

"You don't mind, no?" He looked Langford dead in the eyes before emotionlessly pouring out the whisky.

"I'm here because you're about to make a serious mistake. Denim will not be taken into custody." He swallowed the whisky he coughed and spluttered.

"With all the money I pay you, you drink this piss?!" He exclaimed.

"I'm telling you, the Denim's deaths are best for business, they both know too much to be arrested!" Klichkov finished, he saw the sweat appear on Langford's brow.

"I've already sent a unit." Langford gulped. Fear washed over him just as anger clearly had started to consume Gregor.

"Call them FUCKING OFF! NOW!" Demanded the Russian. That was when Rock stepped into the office.

"There a problem boss?" The behemoth asked starring straight at Langford, murder in eyes. Langford thought he was literally about to shit himself. Gregor didn't answer his giant bodyguard he simply stood up casually walked over to Langford and stated.

"Now!" Signalling to Rock the meeting was over, and now was the time to leave.

Chapter 61

I sat in the darkness washing painkillers down with whisky. Waiting for someone to come crashing through the front door. In two and a half hours no one came. I lit a smoke. As I took down the first hit of nicotine, I heard the window shatter. Then I felt the heat from the bullet across my knuckles as the cigarette disintegrated. Red hot embers were scattered into the air, all in different directions. Instinctively I dropped to the floor, scrambling behind a sofa.

I fumbled through my pockets searching for my phone. I knew it was the same bastard sniper as before! I had to warn Michael and the MI5 mob as this fucker had already shot a number of police officers! I tried Ali's phone first it went straight to voicemail. Michael's phone rang a number of times.

"What's the point, in having a poxy phone if you ain't going to fucking answer it!" I thought out loud before hanging up!

It left me with few options. I could either stay here, behind the sofa, and wait this bastard out or chance getting myself upstairs. The problem was if I waited him out, I was almost certainly sentencing Michael, Ali and the MI5 mob to death, and if I somehow made it upstairs, I was probably dead myself. To make matters worse I'd already taken too long making my decision!

Then I heard sirens, the police were on they're way. I knew that wouldn't stop this bastard, but it might just give Mike and the others a chance. I contemplated just for a second turning my Gloch on myself, but I still had a lot more to do before I could give up. The arrival of the police may also force the sniper's hand. It unsettled me as I realised a second shot hadn't been fired. Maybe the sniper thought he'd slotted me already. In that case the police presence might just have him on his toes. I decided to take the chance. Slowly I made my way through the gloom, crawling out from behind the sofa as I heard the police vehicles, screech to a halt outside the front of the property. The blue lights illuminating the inside of the house, along with me and my position with it! I dove across the room rolling through the door.

I knew the police may have bought me some time, but I still couldn't allow them to arrest me either. I heard more shots from outside. As I'd feared the sniper had now turned his attention to the police! I heard windows shattering, as the sniper peppered the police vehicles in a hail of bullets. I was in no position to help them either, I had to get out. The sniper once he'd finished with the police, he was going to come down to confirm his kill. I heard shouts of armed police as the officers dug in outside. I raced through to the back door into the Priest's back garden. I dove into a bush, as I just saw two armed officers entering the other side of the garden. Sneaky bastards I laid there barely even breathing for fear of being caught.

I remained silent and still until the officers made, they're way into the property. I then leapt from my hiding spot and sprinted down the garden. I vaulted the fence, then placed my Gloch in my waistband. Just yards from me were two more armed officers.

This time both officers clocked me. The gig was up, or was it? Both had police issued pistols trained on me. I placed my hands on the back of my head almost instinctively and marched slowly towards them. One officer placed his pistol into its holster whilst the other kept his aimed at my chest. The officer with the holstered weapon approached me stony faced.

As the officer reached me, he rounded me standing behind as his mate pushed the pistol against my chest. In a flash I grabbed his gun hand pushing it to my right. It was unfortunate he pulled his trigger hitting his buddy in the shoulder. I wrestled the gun from the officer as his partner dropped to the floor in pain and shock. Once I had the weapon in my possession, I slammed the handle into the officer's temple knocking him out.

I relieved both officers of their MP5's, handcuffs, and radio's. Using both sets of handcuffs I cuffed the officers together back-to-back. I located the keys in the vehicle behind them. Activating one of their radios I gave a shout as I jumped in the police van.

"OFFICER DOWN! OFFICER DOWN!" I turned the key slammed the van into first and pulled away tossing the radio's out the window.

Chapter 62

Michael shifted himself awkwardly struggling to fish out his mobile without one of the MI5 agents catching him. After the last time. They were just two minutes from a property owned by the Church of England but registered to a Jonathon Priestly. Michael knew instinctively this was the bastard they'd been chasing. If Jimmy hadn't done it already Michael was going to kill the bastard as clear as it had been from the call that Jimmy had done just that Michael enjoyed the thought for just a moment.

As he did free his phone from his pocket and allowed the screen to light up it revealed several missed calls from Jimmy.

"Shit!" Michael cursed out loud. Victoria fixed him with an accusatory look through her rear-view mirror.

"What?" She asked clearly exasperated.

"Jimmy's been calling. Probably means he's in the wind by now." Michael stated. As he did a police vehicle flew out of the turning that would lead them to the Priest's home. Fuller managed to see it was Jimmy driving.

"That's him, follow that van Vic!" Fuller blurted out. Michael looked at Ali, both men knew this twat had always wanted to say that. The smirk on his face confirmed it.

Victoria ripped up the handbrake before spinning the steering wheel to the right and planting her foot on the accelerator. They caught up with the armed response vehicle in seconds. Victoria flashed her headlights furiously, indicating for the police van to pull over, but Jimmy simply sped up clearly not looking to be arrested. Michael pulled out his phone, dialling Jimmy's number. He answered on the fourth ring.

"I can't talk, I'm driving! Don't go to the address there's a sniper I'll call you when I'm back in London!" Jimmy declared and hung up. Michael sat in shock for a moment before hitting redial. This time it rang off

"Fucking stubborn bastard!" Michael cursed his brother. Victoria gave Michael a soft smile clearly appreciative of his efforts to help.

Victoria slowed following Jimmy from a safer distance. The group discussed going back but ultimately agreed that to close this case they needed to speak to Jimmy. It was a long hour drive back to London with Victoria keeping a two-car distance all the way back. They drove with the radio playing news updates hoping they'd made the right choice in abandoning the police at the Priest's address.

Chapter 63

I drove slowly through London, occasionally speeding up trying to lose the car, which had been following me since I'd got out of the Priest's road. It would've been too dangerous to lose them on the motorway. So, I led them onto an estate I knew, that was like a maze, opening up the van every other turning. It took a further 20 minutes to build a big enough gap to make it a matter of luck for my tail to keep with me but lose them I did. The longer I kept this car the higher my risk of being caught was getting.

I found a small carpark roughly half hours walk from where I needed to be. I bundled the stolen MP5's into a holdall finding a silencer in the back of the vehicle and promptly added it to the bag before setting off. I headed to O'Grady's bar just outside of Croydon. I walked briskly keeping my nut down covering as much of my face as I could from cameras and any other interested party, without looking to suspicious. I had to thank my lucky stars as I found an alley leading to the back of O'Grady's bar.

The alley was scattered with large red Biffa bins, I used for cover as I approached two suit wearing security guys stood outside watching the doors. I knelt down behind one of the bins. Removing one of the MP5's and attaching the suppressor. I slid the holdall under the bin before leaning around the side of the bin and taking my shots.

I hit the first guy head on. The bullet entered his skull through his right eye. His pal clearly in shock reached inside his jacket for something but he was too late I put two in his chest as I stood up running towards him. I slotted the third bullet into his forehead.

I searched the two bodies. The second had definitely been reaching for a gun. They both had been carrying ID cards a bit surprising for gang members but Then I saw the card reader on the door. I walked through the corridor there were four doors two on each side. I opened the first door on the left. It led to a staircase heading down to a cellar. I turned to open the door opposite. I entered into a large office. There behind a massive mahogany desk was the man I was looking for.

Colm O'Grady was an intimidating individual. Even sitting at his desk faced with a MP5 there was no sign of fear on his face. His ginger hair receding down his face to a bushy ginger beard. He wore an extortionately priced green suit, with a white silk shirt with the top button undone. His large frame adorned with gold jewellery.

"And what the fuck do you want?" He asked me in his thick Irish accent. I fixed him with a hard stare my trigger finger already tensing. I could shoot him now; I knew who the main players were but they maybe less helpful. The paddy could be high enough to know who pulled the trigger, but low enough to talk.

"What do you know about my parents?" I questioned ready to pull the trigger if he refused me an answer.

"Oh, you're the Denim boy." He stated in his thick Irish brogue, not an ounce of fear present.

"I suppose that snitch Shawcross sent you in my direction."
He still wasn't answering my question. So, I put a round in
his shoulder.

"Who pulled the fucking trigger? You fucking Paddy cunt!"
The question seethed through my gritted teeth.

"I'm the CUNT! You fucking shot me you psychotic cunt!"
he screamed at me. I arced my weapon in line with his
other shoulder. I saw his eyes widen with fear. I tried to
take advantage.

"Answer the fucking question!" I ordered him.

"You're fucking dead anyway. It just depends how long it
takes me to end you and trust me I'm in no real rush." I
continued before pulling the trigger.

Again, Colm screamed and cursed.

"I know I'm fucking dead, you idiot!" He fixed me with an
evil hard stare there was no emotion in his eyes.

"I ordered the hit you mug!" As he finished the anger
bubbled inside me, I almost shot him repeatedly. Ready to
kill him there then.

"You think you're a gangster? You're a fucking Del Boy
wannabe you cunt!" He berated me. I rounded the table
keeping the gun trained on him. I flicked the weapon to
rapid fire and sent a burst into his legs. Then slammed the
butt of the gun into his knees and then his nose.

"Let's see Del Boy do that!" I told him. I was running out of ways to cause him pain and I was beginning to think he knew it as well. I needed to change tact.

I scanned the room seeing a wall safe. I placed the barrel of my gun on his left foot. Looking him in the eye, I changed my question.

"What's the combination?" Colm's eyes narrowed.

"Get the message I ain't telling you fuck all!" He told me so, I blew his foot off! Colm screamed his eyes streaming locking on the door. He was trying for time the twat thought his security would save him. They might have but he'd given the game away. I knelt down behind him jamming my finger into his right shoulder wound.

His screams did bring the required effect. The four-suit clad bouncers didn't stand a chance. As door flew open, the bouncer's guns in hand looking around the room for their target. I let rip with the MP5 catching them all several times in the chest.

"It could be that easy for you, just give me a name." I told him. He looked at me utterly defeated.

"Sampson Denearez!" He spluttered through the blood now pouring from his broken nose. The defiance slipping back to him he could've taken you out 4 or 5 times now!" He started laughing. I simply took a step back lifted the MP5 leaving him to stare down the barrel.

"Combination now!" I demanded as soon as he gave it to me, I pulled the trigger. The back of his head exploded. I left him slumped in his chair. His blood flowed across his desk.

Pushing the combination into the wall safe. Inside there were rolls of £50 notes and a set of Mercedes keys. I grabbed the keys and pocketed the rolls of notes. I poured petrol over the office, soaking the bodies including those in the hall. I located O'Grady's Merc quickly thanks to his personalised plates. Retrieving the holdall from under the bin. I dumped the MP5 and holdall in the boot, lit a smoke enjoying the dry tickle as the tobacco hit my lungs. Then flicked the lit cigarette in the direction of the bar. I jumped in the Merc and sped off.

Chapter 64

Sampson stroked his beard as he lined up his next shot. He fixed his crosshairs on an older looking officer. The officer was clearly barking orders if Sampson wanted to escape this was the man to take out! Taking out the IC would cause enough confusion for Sampson to take advantage. The pigs had no idea what they'd stumbled into! Sampson pulled the trigger and the commanding officer's head snapped back before he dropped lifeless to the floor.

Officers flocked to their superior's corpse. That was all the opportunity Sampson needed. He rapidly dismantled and packed away his rifle. In a matter of seconds, he was charging through the woodland, back to the road and eventual freedom.

He jumped in the car running his hand through what was left of his black hair. Denim was finally dead! Sampson had redeemed himself. It had taken the best part of a decade, but he'd now done it. He fished out his phone as he drove off. There were only two numbers stored on it, so it didn't take long to locate Colm's number. It had taken a long time to obtain his final shot, against the police and now his boss wouldn't answer his poxy phone.

Sampson drove back to O'Grady's bar. As soon as he pulled up, the feeling of elation was instantly replaced with that sinking feeling of failure! Seeing the flames that had engulfed the bar Sampson knew then Denim had survived. Sampson cursed the police as they had forced him to forego his confirmation check. Now he also had to come to terms with the fact his oldest friend was more than likely now dead.

The anger grew inside him, bubbling just below the surface. Sampson knew soon it would explode like a volcano and he knew it wouldn't be long. He pulled away dialling the second number he had stored in his phone.

$$* \qquad * \qquad *$$

Krueger answered on the second ring. This week kept going from bad to worse. Jimmy fucking Denim just wouldn't die! Everyone below Gregor was growing more and more expendable! And Marcus knew after the call from Sampson it was only a matter of time before Jimmy would come for them all. If Sampson was right and O'Grady was dead, there was only three main players left.

He sat in his lounge chair and switched on the news. This shit with Denim was escalating. He was making this all far too public for Krueger's liking. The organisation wouldn't survive the slightest bit of media speculation. Marcus was dreading the fact he had to call Klichkov to inform him of yet more failure knowing it could very well be the last call he ever made.

*   *   *

Gregor simmered in his large armchair as he placed his burner phone on the table before gulping down a large glass of vodka. His empire was crumbling he could feel it. Just as he was on the brink of a deal that would make him appear untouchably legitimate. He'd always managed to appear this way before however this deal would allow him to launder his money in much vaster quantities. He knew it would work as he'd seen it happen just two years prior.

Another of his countrymen and fellow oligarch had bought a London based football club. Gregor wasn't saying this other Russian was laundering money, but it had made Gregor realise it was the ideal front for his criminal empire.

Gregor was sure after this deal went through; he could launder hundreds of millions a week. Maybe he could even retire this time next year however with the Denim boy still running around he was currently no better off than he was in 1980. As in 1980 there were two options, kill the Denim shaped thorn in his side or face serious prison time. However, this Denim seemed less concerned with handling Gregor over to the authorities but set on putting several bullets in him.

There had only really ever been one choice Gregor was ever going to make. It was time to rally the troops. The order was given Marcus would now set everyone after Denim from the Albanians to the Roadmen. Every dirty bastard in London would be on the hunt. Maybe it was a week too late but there was no way Denim would survive another day!

Chapter 65

I drove a safe distance from O'Grady's before dumping the Merc and calling Mike. I laughed quite hard when he'd explained it had been them who had followed me from the Priest's home. Obviously, I was also very apologetic although it was probably best, they hadn't been involved with O'Grady.

I knew the walls were closing in, I was running out of time. This was confirmed as I walked past a newsagent. Plies of the usual rags with some pointless celeb on the front pages. Then I noticed a small picture of myself. So, I pulled my cap down lifted my collar trying again to cover as much of my face as possible. I walked with my head down taking backstreets and alleyways as and when possible. Unfortunately, this made me a clear target.

I walked for about 40 minutes before the inevitable happened. A small group of youths in hoodies and loose jeans attempted to surround me.

"Easy now Grandad." The clear leader of the group approached me lifting his jacket to reveal a pistol in his waistband.

"What's in the bag?" He continued. I lifted my head to meet his stare.

"You don't want to know." I told him, as I saw a flicker of recognition in his eyes.

"Shit, you're that OG killing all of them old boy gangsters!" He spluttered going for his gun. This had gone south fast. I hadn't wanted to hurt these lads they were only about 16-18 but I wasn't going to die here!

Dropping the holdall, I gripped the gang leader's belt in one hand his gun in the other pushing hard into mates behind him.

"Don't make me do this!" I told him. I noticed him reaching for his back pocket. My gut told me knife so I opened fire. I put two bullets in his gut as he dropped, I stared down his mates.

"Get him to a hospital now!" I told them dropping his gun as I walked away, I hoped he'd make it he was young and from what I'd seen had plenty of prison time waiting for him. Not that I currently had room to talk I owed the public a life sentence at least by this point.

It didn't take long for a car to pull up to my relief it was Mike. The MI5 crew had tracked my phone to find my location. William jumped out the passenger side of the motor.

"Jimmy Denim, look at the fucking state of you!" He exclaimed, the cheeky bastard.

"It's been a rough couple of days sir." I responded. Then Victoria stepped out of the car.

"You can say that again you're in a shit ton of trouble Denim!" She informed me looking as beautiful as ever.

"It's all been self-defence, Ma'am." I lied.

"Burning down a nightclub and blowing up a flat is not what I call self-defence!" She advised me.

"The club and flat I was putting down as a public service." I flashed a cheeky smile, hoping I could charm or at least joke my way out of a prison spell. Nobody laughed.

"So, are you arresting me, or are you going to help me finish this?" I asked hopeful but not expectant.

"We want answers regarding the Priest Jim." It was William who answered me this time.

"If that helps you, I'd be happy with that." He finished. I knew information sharing wouldn't help me now. The people I was dealing with, were above legal reprisals, and normal justice. Any case I built would be quashed by the CPS. I tried to explain this to the pair of MI5s Agents relying on the military minds they must still possess. That's when Michael jumped out the car cursing and threatening arrest himself. Victoria and Ali grabbed Michael leading him away in an attempt to calm him down as me and William tried to work out our options.

"Look Will I know by rights you should arrest me but if you do that the bastards that are left will rebuild and they will continue to get away with everything." And by everything I meant the child murders. This went much deeper than my parents now I needed to end both Marcus and Klichkov for every child they had abused and murdered.

"I get all that Jim I really do but we're not soldiers anymore there are rules to civilian life I think you need reminding of that." He stated in a superior tone I didn't care for. The fucking toffee-nosed wanker.

Chapter 66

Carly had never spent much time away from her father and home. Ray had been a hardman and fiercely protective. It had been clear to everyone that Ray loved his little girl more than anything. Now Carly tried to remember the early days after her mother had died trying to replicate the feeling of strength and security her father had created.

She hadn't spent much time with children either and now here she was with Jimmy's daughter Lacey. Carly had known instantly upon seeing Lacey she would do anything to keep her safe. Now in the safe house Carly kept feeling she might very well have to.

The MI5 Agents had a number of plain clothed armed officers watching them both. Carly looked them when they'd arrived wondering if these men could really keep them safe. Their ages seemed to vary three looking too young to be on the force, cocky and far too excited to have seen any action. Unlike Jimmy who Carly recalled having a cold almost serene air about him when he'd been forced into action. Then there were the two officers who were in their thirties. These officers resembled Jimmy switched on but not excited there simply to do the job and fuck off home to their families. Then there were the two officers on the wrong side of middle age these two had spent the last few hours sat in the kitchen drinking tea and playing cards.

Carly insisted on keeping Lacey close to her. It would be boring for the little mite thought Carly, but she'd feel safer having her there in arms reach. She just couldn't shake the feeling that something was very off with this whole set up. Her gut was screaming take the child and get away from these idiots and their guns! But fear of what was coming made her cling to anything that might keep them safe.

*   *   *

Marcus had, had enough of all the bullshit with the Denims now! He'd spent the entire afternoon inundated with phone calls Jimmy did this Jimmy did that Jimmy killed this person etcetera! Marcus was fast running out of business associates, not to mention patience. Himself and Gregor had always made a conscious effort to keep all the gangs in London separate. Keep them using different suppliers for their drugs. This made it easy to control the prices and allowed them to orchestrate any gang wars when necessary. Marcus had it all worked out the Somalians, Turkish, East London and the Yardies got their shipments through Shawcross. The Nigerians, West London, Albanians and the Triads dealt with O'Grady. Now Marcus was organising meets with every damned would-be gangster and drug dealer in London!

He had it all planned out, the Somalian gang would go to the safe house and lift the girls, that way if Jimmy made it to Marcus, he'd hold the two girl's hostage. That was of course if the Albanians didn't kill him before that! It had taken Marcus longer than he'd anticipated to obtain the location of the safehouse but no where near as long as a civilian would expect. He felt he should have known upon the girl's arrival. Apparently due to Jimmy the house was changed last minute. He really was becoming the bane of Krueger's life.

Sampson had failed him for the last time. It was a shame after all these years but there was very rarely retirement from their line of work.

Marcus sent both the Triads and Nigerians after the Irishman. He'd promised all four gangs a £500,000 shipment if they were successful. This bullshit was getting expensive!

*   *   *

The Somalians were run by Meth a black male in his late 20's. His face was horribly scared on the right-hand side, and he was blind in his right eye, after a boiled sugar water attack whilst he was serving a five stretch in HMP Swaleside. Meth and most of his crew knew Jimmy and of his links to Paulie. Meth actually respected Jimmy he'd had dealings with him during a number of gang wars over the years when one of the other gangs would steal product from each other. Paulie would send Jimmy on to collect the debts.

As the Somalians drove through South Croydon towards the safehouse Meth himself had second thoughts. Jimmy had always played fair yes, he'd killed a few of Meth's boys over debts, but only under Paulie's orders and he never brought family into it. Yet the German who Meth didn't know wanted Jimmy's daughter and bitch snatched up. Now Meth had to work out if £500,000 worth of product was worth Jimmy's wrath. Meth looked at his boys in the large SUV they were his family, and he had a responsibility to put food on their tables, and Meth was at the end of the day a business man with very little time for sentiment. In the end only one thing went through Meth's mind.

"Fuck Jimmy! We need to make that paper!"

*   *   *

The Albanians were run by Besnik and despite getting their stock from O'Grady Besnik knew Jim better than Meth ever would. Sending his crew after Jimmy felt dishonourable. Bes decided to find Jim himself as fond of the man as he was £500,000 worth of drugs was not an opportunity Bes could pass up.

Chapter 67

As we drove through London to the safehouse due to my insistence I found I had an ace up my sleeve to avoid any jail time. As William raced us toward the safehouse I sat back with Ali and Victoria. I took my time disclosing everything I had found on the Priest, Krueger, and Klichkov. Michael had sat in the passenger seat remained stony faced throughout my tale, but Victoria took it all in even offering the get out of jail free card I was obviously in need of. They would help catch Krueger and Klichkov if I went and worked for MI5 apparently, I had proven quite useful to the agency.

I kept feeling my mind drawn to Lacey and Carly something wasn't sitting right. Maybe it was not knowing how many coppers and other high-ranking officials Klichkov had been able to corrupt but there was definitely something fucking wrong!

Then out of nowhere, something hit us! A black Escalade with tinted windows slammed into the passenger side of the MI5 car. The windows shattered on impact covering Michael and Ali in pieces of glass. The force of the collision knocked the car over, onto the driver's side. I managed to steady myself as we went over preventing me from landing on Victoria. Unfortunately for both of us Ali wasn't as quick in distributing his weight. My outstretched arms nearly buckled under his huge frame, before he eased himself off using the seatbelt and window frame.

"Is everyone OK?" Will called pushing down the airbag. Everyone gave him an OK.

Ali had a large cut on the top left of his head I had to get everyone out of this. My ears were ringing but I could still hear the shouting outside. I tried to grab Will as he clambered past Michael searching for an exit. I missed him by a second, I almost collapsed as the shot rang out.

I'd realised it was an ambush instantly unfortunately my old CO hadn't. As soon as he'd lifted his head out of the passenger window, our attacker had opened fire. One shot had been enough. Will would have been dead before he had a chance to realise his mistake.

Victoria screamed as Will's body dropped back into the car landing on Mike. Claret poured from the huge wound on the back of Will's head. Mike scrambled through my dead CO's blood to get the lifeless corpse off of him. I couldn't deal with Will's death at that time, not if the rest of us were going to survive this. None of us had time to acknowledge it. Which I knew would be neigh impossible for Victoria, but I had to force the issue.

I grabbed Ali and pulled away the sunroof cover, Ali used the car seats to brace himself and launched a series of kick to the panel. It seemed to take forever for the sunroof to give way. Once it did Ali and I forced Michael through then Victoria.

"You next buddy!" Ali informed me. I tried to protest it was probably my fault we were in this mess.

"There's no way I'm fitting through there! Take the fucker out and come back for me!" He insisted with a curt nod. I smiled and nodded back drew my handgun and stepped through.

I turned just in time to see Besnik climbing over our car. He was positioning himself to make a kill shot from the window.

"Oi, DICKHEAD!" I shouted my gun trained on him. His gaze met the barrel of my gun a look of defeat washed over him.

"Drop the fucking gun Bes!" I was in no mood to be messing about I'd known Bes a long time. I had considered him a friend this felt like a betrayal. Besnik to his credit followed the instruction unaware of Ali's hand reaching up to retrieve the discarded weapon. After removing the firearm Ali reached out the window grabbing Besnik by the scruff of his shirt. As soon as his left hand had hold of Besnik, I saw him pulled down towards Ali, who then threw a big right hand into Besnik's jaw. The blow was impressive the force made Besnik do his best impression of a Pez dispenser before Ali dragged him inside the car.

The next thing anyone saw was Besnik fly out of the sunroof. He hit the floor hard I barely had time to react myself before Victoria was on him. She straddled his chest resting her knees on his arms, before launching several punches to his face.

"YOU FUCKING BASTARD!" She screamed wailing obscenities like a banshee with every blow. As the attack slowed, I leaned in to help Victoria back to her feet. That was when Victoria pulled her gun from its holster shoving the barrel into Besnik's cheek.

"Give me one good fucking reason not to blow your head off! You fucking scumbag!" She screamed all her professional demeanour washed away with the tears streaming down her face.

"Jim's girls." Was the response Besnik gave her?

My stomach lurched what the fuck did he mean by that. I dragged Victoria away lifting Besnik up and shoved him hard into the wall. I knew I didn't need to do much more, Besnik was broken already.

"What about the girls? Bes!" I asked him calmly.

"Meth's after them, Jim he knows where they are." He informed me completely emotionless. I dropped to my knees it was like all the air had been driven out of me. I felt Victoria place a hand on my shoulder as I looked up at her. Victoria's face hardened there was no emotion in her eyes as she again shoved her gun into Besnik's face. There was no hesitation this time, no questions, no chance to beg for the life he didn't deserve. No, this time Victoria pulled the trigger almost acting on instinct. The back of Besnik's head burst like a balloon and like a poor painter decorated half the wall in claret, brain, and skull fragments.

"Victoria you've got to get me to that safehouse now!" I was begging I had to deal with Meth, again someone I had considered a friend. Victoria starred at me, gave me a look of utter contempt.

"My brother has just been murdered! Because of you! AND SOME BULLSHIT YOU'VE GOT YOURSELF INVOLVED WITH! NOW YOU WANT MY HELP! MY BROTHER'S NOT BEEN DEAD FOR FIVE FUCKING MINUTES! YOU ARROGANT CUNT!" She was getting hysterical, due to shock, but again I couldn't deal with that now, I had to get to my girls, I had to keep them safe!

Chapter 68

The minutes passed like hours. One of the younger officer's had gone quiet, almost nervy. Carly hadn't taken her eyes off him! Officer Vinny Clark had his right hand resting on his pistol, and whilst not having said a word for fifteen minutes, he kept checking his watch, and the windows. He was staring to worry Carly.

Then it happened, blinding headlights filled the windows! All but two Officers jumped up taking positions around the room, Vinny didn't move, neither did Douglas Freeman. An officer in his fifties. Slowly he got to his feet, removing his pistol from its holster. He strode purposely towards the officer he'd been drinking tea with moments ago. In one movement, Doug had his friend of some 15 years in a choke hold and opened fire on one of the officers in his thirties. Almost instantly Vinny had also killed the other officer in the thirty-year age bracket. The other remaining officers stood with bewildered looks of shock on their faces. Vinny and Doug killed them all!

It was all over in moments. Carly had managed to smuggle Lacey behind the sofa. She couldn't help thinking, "fuck I fucking knew it!" That was when the front door opened. The lights from the car filled the doorway, making it impossible to identify the male who had entered the room.

Carly realised very quickly, she didn't want to know the identity of the mystery man, as both killer coppers, had replaced their weapons upon his arrival. That was not a good sign. Then came the words delivered in a calm nonchalant tone.

"Where's Jimmy's bitch and brat?!"

Chapter 69

It didn't take long for the armed police to arrive. I was almost grateful for the latest attempt on my life. If the whole fiasco hadn't cost William, his life it may have been worth my potential arrest. Although I was under no illusions, without William's death I would absolutely be on my way to a police cell! However, the death of her brother had lit a new fire in Victoria.

"I want these bastards, Jimmy!" She informed me and with that she had commandeered an unmarked police car, and once again we were on our way.

A feeling of foreboding grew inside me, as we approached the safehouse. All the lights were out, and there was a large SUV parked outside. Victoria turned out the headlights on our approach, but I already knew the bastards were in there! With my daughter, I also knew they wouldn't be leaving!

I retrieved my Gloch from my waistband and attached the silencer. I looked over and Victoria was passing Ali an MP5 and suppressor after Michael had refused to take it, before prepping her own. With the weapons loaded the three of us exited the car. Slowly we made our way to the house, hugging the treeline.

As we approached the SUV, we saw 3 Somalians waiting, they were clearly armed. I nodded to Ali through the darkness in turn, he placed a hand on Victoria's shoulder. I edged closer to the one closest to us, I drew a tact knife from my sock, before springing up in front of him like a jack in the box. I slammed my empty hand across his mouth, I heard four suppressed pops, before two Somalians hit the floor. Pushing the remaining Somalian into the SUV, sticking him with the tact knife, first in the gut, then chest and finally in his throat. Leaving his lifeless corpse in the motor, I started to make my way to the door. A Somalian exited the house, through the gloom I could just make out he had Lacey, he was quickly flanked by two armed officers. Suddenly I heard a shout from behind me.

"ARMED POLICE, PUT YOUR WEAPONS DOWN! NOW OR WE WILL OPEN FIRE!" It was Victoria. In an instant I'd raised my Gloch aimed at the Somalian's head.

"Put her down!" I tried to keep the desperation out of my voice.

"Fuck you!" shouted the young officer. Victoria didn't hesitate she put two rounds in the youthful copper's face. Ali followed suit as the older officer turned to fire on Victoria. He didn't get a chance to pull the trigger. Ali opened up firing wildly, but incredibly accurate, hitting the old boy in the head numerous times. I held off firing, I didn't want him to drop Lacey, or worse risk hitting her myself, but the fear was pouring off the Somalian bastard now.

"I meant now CUNT!" I demanded, this time he placed her down on her feet, so I could see she was conscious. His eyes fixed on the barrel of my gun, silently pleading for his life. It was too late for that now. A single round landed in his forehead.

I ran over picking Lacey up in a tight embrace. This was the last thing I'd ever wanted her to witness. That was when Michael sprinted from the car, he pulled Lacey from my arms and starred straight into my eyes.

"I didn't see Meth, so you need to get in there and fucking end him!" It was a massive shift, for Michael. There was almost sort of understanding in his voice. He then took Lacey back to the car.

As I walked through the door, my stomach lurched at the scene that confronted me. Meth had CJ on her knees in front of him, with his gun pressed against her forehead. He was tugging at his belt, and spouting obscenities and threats at her.

"You're going to put my dick in your fucking whore mouth, or I'm going to shoot you! You bitch!" He informed her; I already had my Gloch trained on him.

"You can back away from her and put your gun down! You ugly son of a bitch!" I told him coolly, the slightest bit of anger seeping through. He turned to see who would dare speak to HIM in that tone, as he did so he took his gun away from CJ, just long enough for me to put two shots in Meth's ugly mug. It was a sudden and brutal end to what I had considered a mutual friendship, I didn't need to know why Meth had, done what he'd done. In all honesty I didn't care why, the fact he'd done all this was more than enough, for me to end his life happily.

Meth's body hit the floor heavily, CJ leapt from her knees running into my arms. I kissed her hard. Relieved she was OK much like Lacey. The fact of the matter was we very nearly missed Meth, and his boys. It wasn't lost on me either if we had missed them, I may never have seen them again. That was something I couldn't allow to happen! I decided then, I couldn't risk this scenario again. The time had come, I had to get CJ and Lacey out of the country. I knew it was a massive risk, trusting a woman I'd only known a matter of days. Especially as not only was I entrusting her with my life, and over £500,000 in cash, but with everything going on, I was leaving my 6-year-old daughter with a woman, it was dawning on me I didn't really know anything about.

In the end the decision was simple, I needed both out of the country. They had both witnessed far more than I'd ever wanted them to. I should be joining them soon enough anyway. My next stop was Krueger, then kill Klichkov, and live the rest of my life in Florida, in peace. At least that was the plan. I lit a smoke, and thought I needed a fucking drink!

Chapter 70

It had been a long fucking week, for Warren. First, he'd been forced out of his family home, by a violent thug ex-squaddie arsehole. Then he'd been arrested on the word of the cunt's corrupt bastard brother! Then his missus had been murdered, and he knew Jimmy fucking Denim had something to do with it! To top it all off he now found himself beaten, blindfolded and bundled into the back of a van.

Warren had no idea what the hell was going on. What had he done to warrant any of this? He wasn't a bad man; he was a fucking P.E teacher at a junior school for Christ's sake! Yes, he'd knocked his missus about once or twice, but she'd asked for it! It certainly didn't warrant all of this! Maybe Jimmy thought he'd killed her, but if he did Warren thought this would've happened much earlier! What ever this was, and come to think of it, it could just as easily have been Jimmy who had murdered Liz. It wasn't like the bastard didn't have form.

He was building up into a rage. Then the van came to a screeching halt! Warren felt his body thrown across the enclosed space, slamming into the wall between him and the driver's cab, hard. Was it finally over? No chance. He heard the side door of the van fly open, then a voice.

"Out now you useless cunt!" The voice demanded, as a huge hand grabbed Warren by his shoulder, dragging him from the vehicle. He knew instantly he was in woodland, he heard the crunch of dry leaves under his feet. The inevitability of his situation now hit him. There was only one reason to kidnap someone, and drive them into a woods, thought Warren. He knew then he was dead!

They seemed to walk for ages, every footfall taking an eternity. In reality they were probably only walking for five to ten minutes. Then suddenly there came a new voice, this time one he recognised.

"I doubt the blindfold is entirely necessary now." Came the heavily accented German tones, of Marcus Krueger. The sunlight was momentarily blinding, but at least Warren knew who he was dealing with. Even if he didn't know why.

As his eyes adjusted, he noted how smartly dressed his captures were. Marcus as always was dressed immaculately. The German wore a royal blue suit, white shirt with a tie matching the suit, he was also wearing a long brown cashmere coat, and a watch Warren knew would cost more than his car. Then there was Marcus' menacing co-conspirator, a man mountain, who looked totally out of place in his expensive suit, and punk styled mohawk with tattoos adorning either side. This monster hadn't taken his intimidating gaze off warren for even a split second. The pair looked ready for a business meeting, not an undeserved murder of an innocent man.

"Marcus, what is this all about mate?" Warren asked, unsure how to handle the situation, but desperate for answers.

"I'm not your mate, Warren!" His face twisting with malice.

"You and your actions have cost me, and my associates a shit ton of fucking money!" He finished fishing out a pair of leather gloves from his inside pocket.

"Marcus, please I don't know what you mean." He was pleading now.

"I know our wives were friends, but they're both dead now, and that Warren is on you!" Marcus informed him, still prepping himself ready for the kill. Warren stood starring bewildered at Marcus' latest revelation.

"What do you mean? Felicity's dead as well? What happened? Please Marcus what the fuck is going on?!" He was begging now.

"Jimmy fucking Denim!" Marcus stated, but still not answering Warren's questions, which kept coming. Much to Marcus' irritation.

After another ten minutes, of Warren's begging, Marcus snapped.

"You have cost me over a fucking million pounds! All because you couldn't keep your fucking hands to yourself!" He screamed, barely inches from Warren's face.

"I've had to have my wife killed, as well as yours because you had to be a fucking big man, well how fucking big do you feel now?" He stepped back holding out his hand. Rock walked over placing a Desert Eagle into Marcus' grip.

Warren dropped to his knees, clasping his hands together, almost praying to Krueger. It didn't help. Marcus had planned to offer Warren a chance to kill Jimmy, and he'd allow him to continue thieving oxygen, but alas the last ten minutes had proven, what a pussy hole Warren was. A cold malicious smile spread across Krueger's face, as he pulled the trigger.

"Right now, get me back home thank you Rock."

Chapter 71

After an hour organising our next move. In the end
Michael volunteered to go with CJ and Lacey. He wasn't
happy with me, but as he was under investigation after
Kate's death, and knowing his superior was definitely
corrupt, he knew he'd be getting fucked over. He would be
better off out of law enforcement altogether.

After all that we dropped the three of them at Michael's,
so he could pack and collect his car. We also discussed
Victoria organising new IDs for us, after all we were
helping her close her case, and who better than MI5 to
supply new official documents, for our new life in America.

Then I, Ali and Victoria made our way to Krueger's home.
I'd taken note of the layout earlier when Felicity had taken
me back. Upon our arrival I carried out a second quick
reccy, locating the apartments fuse box, I logged it then
headed to an area where I could see into the apartment,
with the aid of a pair of binoculars. The lights were on, but
at first, I saw nobody in there. Then a mohawked monster
stood looking out the window. Shit, he looked bigger than
Ali, he would have to be taken out first. Then out of the
shower room strolled a towel clad Marcus. He didn't look

to much older than he did in the photo. We should hit them now! Marcus appeared completely unprepared for an attack.

I returned to the other two and explained the situation. Then once we agreed as to how to proceed, we prepped weapons, and infra-red goggles Victoria had in her possession. Victoria then passed Ali a handheld radio.

"They have a limited range but should work for this." She told him as I pulled the two MP5's from the holdall.

"We'll call when we're at the door, then you knockout his power." I reiterated the plan to Victoria. She simply nodded in response, not happy she wouldn't get a crack at the bastards herself, but with the size of Krueger's minder, I knew I needed Ali, who himself wouldn't shut up, about how he'd been itching to have a crack at that fella since they'd met at CJ's pub.

Ali and I made our way up to the apartment's front door, we paused. Ali quietly radioed down to Victoria.

"Now!" He whispered into the handset. A few seconds later and all the lights went out. We placed the night vision goggles on; I could already hear Krueger shouting at his minder. I set to work picking the lock. We were in, in a matter of moments. Through the goggles I saw Krueger straight away. As I lined up my shot it dawned on me, I couldn't see his minder.

"JIM, MOVE!" Ali shouted barging me forward. Four rounds flew from my weapon, embedding themselves in the ceiling. I heard the two behemoths crash to the floor behind me.

"FOR FUCK SAKE JIMMY, check your fucking corners!" I thought.

I just saw Krueger vanish through a door. There went the element of surprise. I followed, whilst trying to stay clear of the two heavyweights throwing each other around. I could have shot Ali's opponent, but I knew Ali would never forgive me for getting involved. As horrible as it sounds, I actually wanted to watch, the two monsters slug it out. There were people who would pay hundreds to watch a fight of this calibre. I mean the people that call Mike Tyson, the baddest man on the planet, had never seen fighters like these two.

I rounded the door frame, my MP5 ready in a firing position. The bastard flashed a torch at the doorway, blinding me temporarily. I instinctively opened fire in his general direction, then ripped the goggles from my face. Stepping back towards the doorway, I fired off another burst, as I allowed my eyes to adjust to the light. Marcus tried to capitalize on my momentary blindness, diving over the bed, and approaching behind the door to my right.

*   *   *

The force with which, Rock hit Ali with was incredible, sending him hurtling into a nearby wall. Rock lunged at Ali again, but this time Ali was aware, dodging and landing a big right hand on Rock's jaw. In a flash Ali was behind him, wrestling the monster into a sleeper hold, trying to squeeze, Rock's final breath from him. Although Ali's hulking arms were locked in, tight around Rock's throat, Rock had the height advantage, and Ali couldn't set his legs. It allowed Rock to throw Ali over his shoulder, with a hip-toss. Ali landed on his back, Krueger's TV breaking his fall, and almost his back. Ali's weight fortunately crushed the TV, regardless the pain was excruciating.

Adrenaline flooded Ali's system, he leapt to his feet, instantly charging at Rock. Ali's shoulder connected flush with Rock's solar plexus, nailing a rugby tackle any scrumhalf would be proud of. The force took Rock off his feet, and the pair crashed through a wall.

The two combatants landed in a bathroom. Rock took the brunt of the traumatic landing, falling back first into a toilet. The force of Rock's fall smashed the toilet from it's fixings, flooding the apartment. Ali was first to his feet, scrambling looking for his gun, to finally finish the battle. Rock wasn't down for long himself however and was far from done.

Rock launched into a renewed attack, he would never admit it, but Ali had him rattled, and he had to respect that. He ploughed into Ali, throwing lefts and rights into his opponent's ribs, and kidneys. Rock stepped back looking to kick Ali's head off, but Ali countered by biting Rock's thigh. Ali's mouth filled with the blood of his enemy. Rock screamed in pain, then threw a big right hand. Ali slipped under the incoming blow, his own right hand shooting up gripping Rock's throat, lifting him enough for Ali to slam all of Rock's weight through Krueger's coffee table.

Rock slowly got to his feet, pulling shards of glass from his back and arms. He charged at Ali again, but Ali shifted his weight dodging Rock's latest attack. Rock had put too much into his attack and upon his failure to land it, his momentum took him through Krueger's glass panel door. As he stumbled across the balcony, he knew it was over. Ali had his MP5 trained on Rock's chest. As the bullets struck Rock stumbled backwards falling over the balcony.

*   *   *

Marcus used his left hand to push my MP5 into the wall, following through with a big right hand into my temple. He threw a flurry of punches, but I managed to raise my arm. It cushioned the blows, allowing me to compose myself. I stamped down on his bare foot in my heavy boots, as he staggered back, I got control of my weapon, and drove the butt into his nose. I threw a knee into his gut. Trying to create some space between us, to get a shot off. It didn't work, it might have if I'd had the room to plant a proper kick, but in seconds he had a strong grip on my MP5. With surprising strength, he forced me into the wall. Sliding the MP5 up my chest, level with my throat.

Pressing the gun into my throat, Marcus lifted me up the wall, so my feet were an inch off the floor. I struggled smashing my forearms into his, hoping he'd release his grip, he didn't! I grabbed the weapon, using Krueger as a counterweight, I got my feet on the wall, utilising all the strength I had, I launched us both across the room. As we landed, I smashed my knee into Krueger's groin. He let out an agonised scream and relinquished his grip on the firearm.

I jumped to my feet, stepping back, aiming the barrel at Krueger. Finally, it was over, I had him bang to rights. However, as he rolled around in agony, I couldn't permit him a quick death. This bastard was one of the worst of the worst! And deserved every little cunting thing, I was about to do to him!

I targeted his ability to move. Starting by firing two rounds into both his shoulders. Following up with obliterating his kneecaps. He cried out, with each new wound, I inflicted. With this motherfucker immobilised and not even a remote threat to me. I stepped in close. I placed my foot down on Krueger's ankle. Krueger's scream almost masked the snap of the bone, but I definitely heard it. I could drag this out all fucking night, and this cunt would still deserve more. I could feel my hatred for this piece of shit contorting my face.

"What the fuck do you want?" Krueger screamed. I simply placed my barrel on his other ankle.

"Please, stop you've got the wrong man!" Again, Marcus screamed desperately. I pulled the trigger. His screams filled the room yet again.

"You know who I am, just like I know exactly who the fuck you are! Now this can be over really quick, you just need to tell me where I can find Mr Klichkov!" I informed him.

The cunt laughed at me, so I put a bullet in his gut. He cursed his body already racked with pain.

"Idiot, I'm more likely to go into shock than tell you anything. Dickhead!" He said with a smirk. I smiled back at him.

"I know that too cunt, that's what I'm hoping for, you underestimate how much I want to fucking hurt you!" I informed him coldly and placed the MP5 on the bed. I drew a commando knife from my ankle holster. The blade was 6 inches long, and I drove it through his right hand.

It didn't take long, for him to call me every name under the sun, not that I cared. I was genuinely enjoying violently extracting my revenge, the pain he'd earned over the last 30 years, at least. I knew, I wouldn't get much in the way of information from Marcus, but I didn't need it. We would find Klichkov when we needed to.

Victoria's contacts were already tracking his movements and locating all his known address'. I yanked the blade from his hand, then slammed it down on his fingers, taking three off his hand. Ali walked in, his radio in hand.

"Jim, what the fuck are you doing?" Ali shouted, not even attempting to hide his shock. I realised then I was enjoying all this too much. I was becoming like all of these bastards.

I drew my Gloch from my waistband, held it to Marcus' head.

"Go to hell you piece of shit!" I told him, he looked at me defiantly.

"Pussy!" He spat, as I pulled the trigger.

"Turn the power on Vic." Ali radioed down removing his goggles. He fixed me with a disapproving stare, as the room illuminated.

"I know, but the cunt deserved it, in fucking spades!" I stated.

"And how many times could we have looked at the enemy like that Jim?" Ali asked, his face and voice softening.

"We've got to be better than them." He added. I knew he was right, but it didn't mean I had to like it!

Chapter 72

Michael opened his front door, and instantly sensed something was wrong. He was thankful he'd handed his car key to CJ, and she'd taken Lacey to wait in the motor. #he could feel the danger in the air. There was someone in his house, waiting in the dark. Michael was filled with terror, but also determined to survive. Putting his fear to the back of his mind, embarrassing a steely calm, now hunting his would-be assailant. The unfortunate thing was Michael was practically unarmed, all be it for his pava spray, and baton. Whilst the cunt waiting in the darkness, would most definitely be better prepared!

Michael prepped his police issued arsenal, whilst trying his hardest to reduce the sound of his movements. All the while listening for tell-tale signs, which may give away the arseholes position! There was nothing, until Michael entered his living room.

The sound rightfully filled Michael with debilitating dread! It was a sound almost everyone could identify in a second, it would have been heard through millions of TV screens, millions of times, but only a few would have heard it in this situation. The sound of a pistol being cocked was terrifying! Especially as it had come from behind Michael in the hallway! It left Michael with very few options. Instinctively he spun around unloading his CS spray in his would-be killer's face.

Then shock took hold, the barrel was an inch from his nose! That being said it was the man holding the gun, which had confused Michael. DCI Des Langford, his face burning red, through rage and the effects from the CS spray. If by some small miracle he survived this, Michael would really need to re-evaluate his character judgement skills. The two officers he'd trusted implicitly, had both been bent!

Michael slammed his baton, against Langford's gun toting forearm. Whilst side stepping, trying to avoid the barrel. It nearly worked, but Langford was quicker on the trigger, then Michael had hoped. The gun was louder than Michael had anticipated. It disorientated him for a second. Until the bullet hit. A searing pain ran through Michael's left shoulder. Instinctively his left hand dropped his pepper spray. Through the pain Michael swung his baton in a Z shape. The baton slammed into Langford's left knee, before smashing into his right elbow and shattering his left shoulder. Langford screamed howling expletives in agony.

Michael felt his shirt getting wet, and he realised he was losing a lot of blood. He'd gone into shock. Slowly he staggered backwards, before falling on his arse. Des rubbed frantically at his eyes, his vision still impaired by the CS spray. His knee could be broken, the pain was unbearable! Langford scrambled for the gun, trying to find it through touch alone.

*   *   *

CJ heard the shot ring out. For a second, she found herself frozen by fear, until she saw Lacey. She saw the fear and shock wash over the child's face. She had to do something, even if as she thought the worst had happened, Carly knew she would have two choices, stay in the car, and die here helpless, or she could fight. There was very little chance of survival either way, but she was a Valentine, and she knew what her father would've done.

Carly made Lacey laydown in the footwell, in the back of the car, and laid a discarded jacket on top of her.

"No matter what happens don't move until I get back." She told the young girl. With as much calmness as she could manage. Then as quietly as she could she shut Lacey in the car, and made her way into the house, picking up a pot plant on her way.

She soon realised she'd made the right choice. There in the hallway, was an older man, his hand held out holding a gun! Carly launched the pot plant with as much force as she could at the man's head. It smashed over the bastard's bonce. It wasn't enough, luckily for her the man was clearly disorientated, and he did drop the gun. She rushed him, grabbing him by what little hair he had, and kneeing him in the head repeatedly.

CJ's arrival, and lifesaving attack, gave Michael a new impetus on survival. He jumped to his feet, then slowly, as if he were thinking hard on what to do, he picked up the gun. Again, he approached Des and Carly, fighting the voice in his head. Fighting the voice that was screaming at him, to "SHOOT THE BASTARD!" It was a fight he would lose, but first he needed answers!

"How fucking long!?" Michael asked, placing the barrel on Des' forehead. He struggled to keep his hand steady.

"You ain't got the stones Denim!" Was Des' response.

"How long have they had you in their fucking pockets?!" Mike wasn't giving in. He knew he was going to have to kill the man. A man he'd looked up to up until all this shit started.

"They put me in the force to begin with! You thick cunt!" Des was smiling now; in fact, he was almost laughing.

"Not that you'll ever prove fucking any of it, no matter how long you spend in your cell thinking about it. Oh, that's right Denim, we've investigated Kate's death, and there's a warrant out for your arrest. Suspicion of murder!" Now he was laughing and laughing hard!

Michael took a moment for that information to sink in. Then he indicated for CJ to head back to the car. Before turning his attention back to Langford.

"Well then what's the harm in another!" Michael stated coldly. Des' eyes widened as he realised, he was about to die.

"I hope you'll accept this as my resignation." To his surprise when the time came to pull the trigger, Michael didn't freeze. He didn't even hesitate. His tigger finger moved with a determined purpose. Michael dropped the gun, disgusted with himself, Langford had deserved it, but he shouldn't of done it! He knew he was just as bad as Jimmy now. Any moral high ground he had once held was now lost.

He had to force himself to snap out of his melancholy, he still had everything he'd come for! And if he was in fact wanted for murder get away from his home address before more officers arrived.

Chapter 73

It had been hours since I'd finally ended Krueger's miserable life. True to her word, Victoria had provided alternative passports for me and Michael. Michael had called to inform us of his need of a new identity. Following the murder of DCI Langford, he now feared he had two warrants out for his arrest.

Victoria had left us to meet up with Michael and the girls, to make sure all three of them made it out of the country safely. She gave me a stern look.

"Leave Klichkov, until I get back!" Was the last thing she said. Almost as if I was going to listen.

Ali and I couldn't help ourselves. We knew where he was going to be and when he'd be there.

"We could always run a bit of recon." Ali had suggested, I agreed whole heartedly. If the Russian and his mob, decided to engage we couldn't possibly be held accountable. I'm sure Victoria would see things differently, but that was a problem for later.

It was early morning when we arrived, outside the football stadium, Gregor was due in just over an hour. The place was alive with activity already. We decided to watch the main entrance from a small café across the street. I was starving so again we agreed a full English was in order.

I was halfway through my third cup of tea, when a black Bentley Continental, with tinted windows, abruptly pulled up outside the stadium's main entrance. This was it! I downed the remainder of my brew and gave Ali a nudge. I got up placing a reddy on the table, giving the waitress a quick nod before we ran for the door. I felt my eyes narrow, as Klichkov exited the chauffeur driven, luxury motor. It was too late now there was no way I was waiting for Victoria!

Ali and I made our way to the car, and loaded up, if you could call it that. The makeshift car boot "armoury" was nearly thread bare. I grabbed the MP5 with only 8 rounds left in the mag. With a silencer attached it would be worth having for an initial assault. Next, I lifted my Gloch and screwed on the suppressor. There were only a handful of rounds left in that as well. Ali went another way grabbing a shotgun there was an abundance of ammo for it, but it only held 6 rounds at a time, and was going to make a hell of a racket. Ali always had been about as subtle as a house brick to the face. Ali then picked up a pistol and number of tactical knives.

We watched as two more cars pulled up, clearly Klichkov's security detail. They filled the stadium foyer. There were 8 men in total, and I couldn't help but worry what we had missed getting out of Klichkov's car whilst we got loaded up! The 8 men we had seen looked seriously professional all of them were in high-end designer suits and sunglasses. Each also had those covert radio earpieces. I couldn't help but think our security firm was a bit basic.

We followed slowly making our way to the foyer. Ali opted to use his side arm first and attached a silencer. I was grateful for that. As soon as he started letting off with that shotgun, the police would be well on their way! Meanwhile I readied my MP5 flicking it to single shot. I felt sorry for the young girl working the front desk. The look on her face was one of pure horror, as we entered. The terrified secretary was accompanied by a large man in a suit. He reached inside his jacket with one hand, whilst raising his other to his mouth clearly trying to radio his buddy's and inform them of our arrival. He wasn't fast enough! Ali put two rounds in his nut, giving me a cheeky nod after, first blood to Ali.

I applied the safety to my MP5 and allowed it to hang by my side as I approached the girl who still sat traumatised at the desk. I walked over with my hands open, and palms outstretched. I knelt down beside her and began reassuring her. Ali meanwhile secured the rest of the room.

I know the secretary would know what Klichkov was doing here, and more importantly where he would be. Due to the invaluable information this young girl held I had to get her onside and fast.

"It's alright miss, we're here to stop them." I told her hoping she'd see the truth. She was a nice looking girl, her brown hair pulled back in a bun. She was dressed in a black business suit, with the club crest embroidered on the blazer. It was a very professional look with the white blouse underneath.

"What's your name darling?" I asked keeping my voice soft but assured.

"Nicole." She answered, the shock and fear evident in her voice.

"OK Nicole. I'm Jim and this is Ali. We need to know where Mr Klichkov is." I said again softly but with the confidence to help put her at ease. I continued to reassure her, softly and slowly.

Something I said must have worked, as she not only told me where to find Klichkov, but she also gave me directions on how to get there. This was it now! I placed a hand on Nicole's shoulder.

"Thank you." I told her with a grateful smile. Upon Ali's quick search of the dead security officer, we realised, most if not all these cunts were going to be armed.

We headed off, following Nicole's directions. Zig zagging up the hallways. Both of us keeping low. It was all going so well we were however starting to wonder where all the security was, we didn't have to wait long to find out. As we rounded the corner, we spotted four stood outside the chairman's office. I pulled Ali back, there had to be a way for one of us to get round the other side, so we could turn this hallway into a kill box. I mimed the idea to Ali. He nodded in agreement, and I set off.

Keeping low I headed back to the last corridor running parallel to the chairman's office. The stadium wasn't hard to navigate. Within ten minutes, I'd circled the office. From the other side of the Russian wanker's security, I could see Ali getting agitated. He kept poking his head round the corner. He was lucky he hadn't been spotted, or worse. I rounded the corner I fired off four shots, hitting two of the bastards both head shots. As I ducked back round the corner, I heard two, tell-tale pops, as Ali dispatched the other two.

Slowly we converged on the office door. Ali placed the pistol back in his wristband, gripping the shotgun he charged at the door kicking the handle the door flung open. My heart sank as quick as the bullets struck Ali. I saw at least 8 land, I shoved him away letting off the last 4 rounds in the MP5. I hit two gunmen fatally. I missed the third. Instantly I grabbed my Gloch and tossed the MP5, I dove back trying to avoid the incoming volley of bullets, letting off a few of my own! I felt a round burn down my right cheek, taking the top of my ear with it. He was firing wildly, as another round hit my left calf. I managed much better, hitting him with 4 rounds. One to the chest, one in his throat, and two in the face! I landed on my back, suddenly I realised again I hadn't checked the fourth corner. I jumped to my feet, the pain in my calf almost forced me back to the floor. I lifted my Gloch level with Klichkov's forehead.

That's when checking my corners came back to haunt me. Haunt being the operative word!

"Jimmy stop." I recognised the voice immediately, and it floored me quicker than any bullet would have! As I turned around keeping my gun trained on Gregor, I felt all the blood drain and I thought my stomach was going to fall out my arse! I was suddenly confronted by a face I hadn't seen in 7 years, a face I never imagined I'd ever see again outside of her photograph. In a split second my entire life had been turned upside down. The woman stood in front of me was ANGELA!

I'd been completely disorientated, especially as my 11-year-old son, who again I had thought was dead, was stood behind his mother! The world seemed to freeze; time had stopped! Until that was Angela's right hand sprung from her side. I felt the blade, cut in my side just below my ribs. I staggered backwards.

"Why can't you just let things go Jim?" Angela asked as if this was all my doing!

"I thought you were dead! What the fuck is going on?" I actually asked out loud, I couldn't make sense of anything. My head was spinning I was dying, and I had no idea how this had gone so fucking sideways.

"Angie, is one of my best operatives." Gregor piped up and informed me as she loomed over me menacingly.

"She gave us invaluable intel on you. It's funny all the time she spent with you, you never seemed to find out about your parents! Now you've decimated my business! And for what? My favourite assassin is going to kill you." He informed me.

"You die, and for what? What have you really achieved?" He asked glaring at me.

"Well, I fucked you're shit up, didn't I?!" It was all I could think to say at least I'll piss him off even if it was with my last breath!

I swallowed hard waiting for Angela to strike my final blow. My life didn't flash before my eyes, I just felt a wave of defiance wash over me! Suddenly everything Angela had done sank in, she'd faked her own death and taken my son. I glared at her, all these years I'd put her on a pedestal now there was nothing but hatred towards the bitch. She didn't hold my stare for long.

A loud explosion filled the room Angela stopped like a deer in headlights. Slowly she looked down towards where her midriff used to be. I turned to the door Ali was sat leaning against the wall, smoke seeping from the barrel of his shotgun. I instinctively spun to my feet raising my Gloch in one movement, the pain was immense, but I stood barrel back on Klichkov's forehead. However, this time there was a gun in my face! Neither of us hesitated pulling our triggers simultaneously

I nearly laughed, his gun did nothing mine simply clicked I was out of ammo, his had jammed! Thinking fast I kicked him in the chest, with my injured leg. He fell backwards, and Ali who was now fading fast threw the shotgun to me. I cocked the pump handle, now standing over the Russian. I lowered the weapon to his face.

"Smile you son of a bitch!" I said pulling the trigger, quoting the final line of my favourite movie character, Chief Brody. Klichkov's head seemed to vanish, into a sea of claret.

I staggered around the room, I wanted to drop, I was exhausted, but I was filled with concern. Bexley had witnessed everything, but he had simply stood and watched. Even now there was no emotion on his face. I knew without looking Ali was gone. I'd feel the guilt of his death for the rest of my life, however short that maybe.

Epilogue

6 months later

Life was good I thought as I sat on my new deck, overlooking the California hills. I lit a smoke and took a sip of whisky. This time for pleasure, and not as a stress relief. I'd definitely left all the stress in London. Despite having to completely start over, we'd all started to thrive in California. It had been hard, with straightening things out with Victoria probably being the hardest part. She had been understandably pissed, but ultimately accepting that we had got the result that was required.

I had, had to acknowledge, how none of this would have been possible without Victoria's help. She had single handedly liquidated all of our assets, and organised Carly's inheritance along with mine and Michael's. The three of us were now multi-millionaires, despite the amount MI5 had "confiscated" under the proceeds of crime act. So, Carly and I had bought our 4-bed property in a small town called Topanga, and a bar on Malibu beach. The bar all but ran itself, largely down to the bar manager we had hired. Matt Gilmore was a 30-year-old ex-US-Marine. We'd hit it off during his interview, both being ex-military, but also because he was incredibly enigmatic. Bexley idolised the man, Matt was a great guy, very serious when it came down to security, but when it came down to let his hair down, he was into everything an 11-year-old boy would find incredibly cool.

I'd enrolled Bexley and Lacey in a great school and got Bexley a highly rated psychologist. He had some issues, which was to be expected, but I was both surprised and proud to be able to say my son had adapted to life with us in Topanga brilliantly. The same was true for Lacey, they're teachers had been impressed with their intelligence and physical ability.

Michael had brought himself an apartment, just, outside of Topanga, along with a mechanic business in Bel Air. Although he wanted little to do with me, he didn't want to lose touch with the kids. So tolerated my existence, it wasn't ideal, but it would do for now.

All in all, the stress of the last decade, in the English capitol had now all been worth it. So, I sat on my deck, enjoying the Californian sun, the whisky, and my view of the hills. CJ laying out next to me doing the same, in a tiny bikini, she was magnificent, as I said life was good.

That was until my phone lit up. I answered on the third ring. I was confronted by a male with an Irish accent.

"Jimmy Denim, you're a hard man to find." I was informed by the disembodied leprechaun!

"Who the fuck is this?!" I demanded, although I was fairly sure who I was dealing with.

"Is that any way to talk to an old friend? I'm sat in what I believe is your bar, be here within the hour." Sampson said before hanging up. I decided to follow his order. So, after providing CJ with a brief explanation. I set off for Malibu beach.

The drive down took about 20 minutes. Then came what I loved about living in the states, the right to bare arms! I gave my Magnum a once over, placed it in my shoulder holster, and entered the bar. I spotted Sampson instantly. He sat at a table; he was facing me as I approached. He sat at a table, he was clearly relaxed a fresh pint sat on the table, as he puffed away on a large Cuban cigar.

He stood up as I reached the table. Then raised his hands in a gesture of innocence, then pulled out a pistol, and slowly placed it on the table. Matt stood behind the bar, gave me a concerned look, I gestured for him to stand down. Before I followed Sampson's lead, placing my Magnum next to his weapon. He whistled through his teeth.

"Impressive piece of equipment." He commented, in his Irish brogue, offering his hand to shake.

"What do you want Denearez?" I asked my eyes narrowing.

"I come in peace. I hope to leave the same way." He stated, as I tried to gauge his angle.

"I know and understand you don't trust me. I killed your parents, and I've tried to kill you several times, five times in fact." The Irishman paused, almost trying to work out how I was reacting to this information. I indicated to Matt to bring me a pint over.

"Maybe we should take a seat." I told Sampson, lighting a cigarette, and taking the afore mentioned seat.

We sat discussing what I can only describe as a cease fire between us. Sampson explaining, he had no knowledge of what his employers were really into he'd never been concerned it was simply about the money for him.

"You've kept me employed for the last decade. I'm honestly not sure if it's luck, you being that much better than me, or if I'm getting too fucking old." He chuckled sipping his beer. I didn't find him that amusing but I was willing to accept a mutual respect for the sake of my family.

After an hour, Sampson placed a briefcase on the table.

"For damages. I mean it Jimmy, I'm sorry for the pain I've caused you over the years and I respect you for agreeing to bygones and all that." He informed me; I could only bring myself to offer a curt nod in acknowledgement. With that he picked up his gun and headed for the door. He didn't make it out!

Michael stood in front of him, holding a Smith and Wesson outstretched. Sampson didn't stand a chance as Michael fired a single round point blank into Sampson's face! The back of his head exploded sending pieces of his brains and skull all over my bar! And just like that I thought it was all over! Then I heard Matt on the phone to the police. Reeling off a cover story, before destroying the CCTV. Saving Michael and my liquor license all in one foul swoop.

Special thanks to Kayleigh, Simon, Emma, Ralph, Ian, Ryan and all the OSG's at HMP Rochester.

Printed in Great Britain
by Amazon

86988671R00159